THE HOUSE WITH A CLOCK IN ITS WALLS

"Newly orphaned, Lewis is a plump ten-year-old who has come to live with his Uncle Jonathan; he finds himself very much at home in the old, odd mansion and he quickly becomes fond of both Uncle Jonathan and his next-door neighbor . . . Mrs. Zimmermann. But there's something odd going on: the ticking noise in the walls of the house, the strange things Uncle Jonathan does; Lewis discovers that his uncle has magic powers, that he himself has acquired some occult ability, and that there is a major power struggle between their well-meant white magic and the dire plans of an extinct (but haunting) former owner. Black magic against white, good against evil, the mood and suspense are artfully created and the illustrations exactly right for the eerie tale."

— *Bulletin of the Center for Children's Books*

"What the author has done that's so special is to touch both the intellect and the feelings. He has dusted off the paraphernalia of ancient magic and made us newly aware of the differences between good and evil. His dialogue goes snap, crackle, and pop. He sets chilling scenes with suspense that tightens like a screw. . . . *The House With a Clock in Its Walls* will cast its spell for a long time."

— *The New York Times Book Review*

THE HOUSE
WITH A CLOCK
IN ITS WALLS

JOHN BELLAIRS
pictures by Edward Gorey

Puffin Books

PUFFIN BOOKS
Published by the Penguin Group
Penguin Putnam Books for Young Readers,
345 Hudson Street, New York, New York 10014, U.S.A.
Penguin Books Ltd, 80 Strand, London WC2R ORL, England
Penguin Books Australia Ltd, Ringwood, Victoria, Australia
Penguin Books Canada Ltd, 10 Alcorn Avenue, Toronto, Ontario, Canada M4V 3B2
Penguin Books (N.Z.) Ltd, 182-190 Wairau Road, Auckland 10, New Zealand
Penguin Books Ltd, Registered Offices: Harmondsworth, Middlesex, England

First published in the United States of America by The Dial Press, 1973
Published in Puffin Books, 1993

27   29   30   28   26

Text copyright © John Bellairs, 1973
Illustrations copyright © Edward Gorey, 1973
All rights reserved

LIBRARY OF CONGRESS CATALOGING-IN-PUBLICATION DATA
Bellairs, John.
The house with a clock in its walls / by John Bellairs;
illustrated by Edward Gorey.   p.   cm.
Sequel: The figure in the shadows.
Summary: A boy goes to live with his magician uncle in a mansion
that has a clock hidden in the walls which is ticking off the
minutes until doomsday.
ISBN 0-14-036336-X
[1. Magic—Fiction.]   I. Gorey, Edward, 1925–2000 ill.   II. Title.
[PZ7.B413Ho   1993]   [Fic] — dc20   92-26794

Printed in the United States of America
Set in Janson Text No. 55

For Priscilla, who lets me be myself

The House
with a Clock in Its Walls

CHAPTER ONE

Lewis Barnavelt fidgeted and wiped his sweaty palms on the seat of the bus that was roaring toward New Zebedee. The year was 1948, and it was a warm, windy summer evening. Outside, that is. Lewis could see the moonlit trees tossing gently beyond his window, which was sealed shut like all the windows on the bus.

He looked down at his purple corduroy trousers, the kind that go *whip-whip* when you walk. He put his hand up and rubbed it across his hair, which was parted in the middle and slicked down with Wildroot Cream Oil. His hand was greasy now, so he wiped it on the seat again. His lips were moving, and he was saying a prayer. It was one of his altar-boy prayers:

Quia tu es Deus fortitudo mea; quare me repulisti, et quare tristis incedo, dum affligit me inimicus?

For Thou O God art my strength; why have you cast me off, and why do I go sorrowful, while the enemy afflicts me?

He tried to remember more prayers, but the only one he could come up with was another question:

Quare tristis es anima mea, et quare conturbas me?

Why art thou sorrowful O my soul, and why do you trouble me?

It seemed to Lewis that all he could think of these days were questions: Where am I going? Who will I meet? Will I like them? What will happen to me?

Lewis Barnavelt was ten years old. Until recently he had lived with his parents in a small town near Milwaukee. But his father and mother had been killed suddenly one night in an auto accident, and now Lewis was on his way to New Zebedee, the county seat of Capharnaum County in the state of Michigan. He was going to live with his Uncle Jonathan, whom he had never met in his life. Of course, Lewis had heard a few things about Uncle Jonathan, like that he smoked and drank and played poker. These were not such bad things in a Catholic family, but Lewis had two maiden aunts who were Baptists, and they had warned him about Jonathan. He hoped that the warnings would turn out to be unnecessary.

As the bus rounded a curve, Lewis looked at his reflection in the window next to his seat. He saw a moony fat face with shiny cheeks. The lips on the face were moving. Lewis was saying the altar-boy prayers again, this time with the wish that they might make Uncle Jonathan like him. *Judica me Deus* . . . Judge me O God . . . no, don't judge me, help me to live a happy life.

It was five minutes to nine when the bus pulled up in front of Heemsoth's Rexall Drug Store in the town of New Zebedee. Lewis got up, wiped his hands on his trousers, and tugged at the enormous cardboard suitcase that hung out over the edge of the metal rack. Lewis's father had bought the suitcase in London at the end of World War II. It was covered with ripped and faded Cunard Line stickers. Lewis pulled hard, and the suitcase lurched down onto his head. He staggered back across the aisle with the suitcase held perilously in the air; then he sat down suddenly, and the suitcase landed in his lap with a *whump*.

"Oh, come on! Don't kill yourself before I have a chance to meet you!"

There in the aisle stood a man with a bushy red beard that was streaked in several places with white. His Big Mac khaki trousers were bulged out in front by his pot belly, and he was wearing a gold-buttoned red vest over a blue work shirt. Lewis noticed that the vest had four pockets; there were pipe cleaners sticking out of the top two, and a chain of paper clips was strung between the lower pair. One end of the chain was hooked to the winding knob of a gold watch.

Jonathan van Olden Barnavelt took his steaming pipe out of his mouth and held out his hand.

"Hi, Lewis. I'm your Uncle Jonathan. I recognized you from a picture your father once sent me. Welcome to New Zebedee."

Lewis shook hands, and noticed that the back of Jonathan's hand was covered with a springy mat of red hair. The coat of hair ran right up his sleeve and disappeared. Lewis wondered if he had red hair all over his body.

Jonathan hefted the suitcase and started down the steps of the bus.

"Good Lord, what a monster! It ought to have wheels on the bottom. Unh! Did you pack some of the bricks from your house?"

Lewis looked so sad at the mention of his house that Jonathan decided to change the subject. He cleared his throat and said, "Well, now! As I was saying, welcome to Capharnaum County and beautiful, historic New Zebedee. Population six thousand, not counting . . ."

A bell overhead began to strike the hour.

Jonathan stopped talking. He froze on the spot. He dropped the suitcase, and his arms hung limp at his sides. Lewis, frightened, looked up at him. Jonathan's eyes were glazed.

The bell continued to toll. Lewis looked up. The sound was coming from a tall brick steeple across the street. The arches of the belfry made a howling mouth and two gaping eyes; below the mouth was a large, glowing clock face with iron numerals.

Clang. Another stroke. It was a deep-throated iron bell, and its sound made Lewis feel hopeless and helpless. Bells like that always did. But what was wrong with Uncle Jonathan?

The tolling stopped. Jonathan broke out of his trance. He shook his head convulsively, and with a jerky motion raised his hand to his face. He was sweating profusely now. He mopped his forehead and his streaming cheeks.

"Hmh . . . hah! Hrumph! Ooh! Sorry, Lewis, I . . . I just remembered that I had . . . that I had left a kettle boiling on the stove. I always phase out like that when I remember something I've forgotten, or vicy versy. Bottom of the pot's probably ruined by now. C'mon. Let's get moving."

Lewis looked hard at his uncle, but he said nothing. Together, the two of them started to walk.

They left the brightly lit Main Street, and before long they were trotting briskly down a long, tree-lined avenue called Mansion Street. The overhanging boughs made Mansion Street into a long rustling tunnel. Pools of lamplight stretched off into the distance. As they walked, Jonathan asked Lewis how his schoolwork was coming, and whether he knew what George Kell's batting average was this year. He told him that he would have to become a Tiger fan now that he lived in Michigan. Jonathan did not complain any more about the suitcase, but he did stop frequently to set it down and flex his reddened hand.

It seemed to Lewis that Jonathan talked more loudly in the darkness between the streetlights, though why he did this Lewis couldn't say. Grownups were not supposed to be afraid of the dark, and anyway this was not a dark, lonely street. There were lights on in most of the houses, and Lewis could hear people laughing and talking and slamming doors. His uncle was certainly a strange person, but he was strange in a likable way.

At the corner of Mansion and High, Jonathan stopped. He set down the suitcase in front of a mailbox that said: FOR DEPOSIT OF MAIL ONLY.

"I live at the top of the hill," said Jonathan, pointing up.

High Street was well named. Up they went, leaning forward and plodding slowly. Lewis asked Jonathan several times if he could carry the suitcase, but each time Jonathan said, no, thanks, he could manage it. Lewis began to be sorry that he had packed all those books and lead soldiers.

When they got to the top of the hill, Jonathan set down the suitcase. He took out a red bandanna handkerchief and mopped his face with it.

"Well, there it is, Lewis. Barnavelt's Folly. What do you think of it?"

Lewis looked.

He saw a three-story stone mansion with a tall turret on the front. The whole house was lit up, downstairs, upstairs, and upper upstairs. There was even a light in the little oval window that was set, like an eye, in the bank of shingles at the top of the turret. In the front yard grew a large chestnut tree. Its leaves rustled in the warm summer breeze.

Jonathan was standing at parade rest, his hands behind him, his legs wide apart. Again he said, "What do you think of it, Lewis? Eh?"

"I love it, Uncle Jonathan! I've always wanted to live in a mansion, and this is sure some mansion!"

Lewis walked up to the frilly fence and touched one of the iron pompons that ran in a row along the top. He stared at the sign that spelled out "100" in red glass reflectors.

"Is it real, Uncle Jonathan? The house, I mean."

Jonathan glanced at him strangely. "Yes . . . yes . . . yes, of course it is. It's real. Let's go inside."

Jonathan lifted the loop of shoestring that held the gate shut. The gate squeaked open, and Lewis started up the walk. Jonathan followed close behind, lugging the suitcase. Up the front steps they went. The front hall was dark but there was a light at the far end of it. Jonathan set down the suitcase and put his arm around Lewis.

"Come on. Let's go in. Don't be bashful. It's your house now."

Lewis walked down the long hall. It seemed to take forever. At the other end he emerged into a room full of yellow light. There were pictures in heavy gilt frames on the walls; there was a mantelpiece covered with a wild assortment of junk; there was a big round table in the middle of the room, and over in the corner was a gray-haired woman in a baggy purple dress. She was standing with her ear to the wall, listening.

Lewis stopped and stared. He felt embarrassed. It was as if he had walked in on someone who was doing something he shouldn't be doing. He thought that he and Jonathan had made a good deal of noise coming in, but it was very apparent that the lady, whoever she was, had been surprised when he entered the room. Surprised and embarrassed, like himself.

Now she straightened up, smoothed her dress, and said cheerfully, "Hi there. I'm Mrs. Zimmermann. I live next door."

Lewis found himself staring into one of the wrinkliest faces he had ever seen. But the eyes were friendly, and all the wrinkles were drawn up into smile lines. He shook hands.

"This is Lewis, Florence," said Jonathan. "You remember Charlie writing about him. The bus was on time for a change. They must have gotten the driver drunk. Hey! Have you been stealing any of my coins?"

Jonathan walked over to the table. Now Lewis noticed that the red checkered tablecloth was covered with heaps and stacks of coins. All kinds of coins, most of them foreign. Doughnut-shaped Arabian coins with Boy Scout knots all over them; a heap of dark-brown copper coins, all of which were stamped with the picture of a bald man who wore a handlebar moustache. There were big heavy English pennies that showed Queen Victoria in various states of chinniness, and there were tiny silver coins no thicker than your fingernail. There was an egg-shaped Mexican silver dollar and a genuine Roman coin, covered with green rust. But most of all, in shiny golden stacks, were brass coins with *Bon Pour Un Franc* printed on them. Lewis liked the phrase, and since he didn't know any French, it got twisted around in his mind till it came out *Bon Sour One Frank*.

"No, I have not been stealing any of your precious Brasher doubloons," said Mrs. Zimmermann in an irritated voice. "I was just straightening up the stacks. Okay, Brush Mush?"

"Straightening up the stacks. I've heard *that* one before, Hag Face. But it doesn't matter, because we're going to have to divvy up the coins three ways. You play poker, don't you, Lewis?"

"Yes, but my dad won't . . ." He stopped. Jonathan saw tears in his eyes. Lewis choked down a sob and went on, "My . . . my dad wouldn't have let me play for money."

"Oh, we don't play for money," said Mrs. Zimmermann, laughing. "If we did, this house and everything in it would belong to me."

"Poop, it would," said Jonathan, shuffling the cards and puffing clouds of smoke from his pipe. "Poop, it would. Get 'em all divided up, Frumpy? No? Well, when you're ready it's going to be dealer's choice, and I'm the first dealer. No ladies' games, like Spit-out-the-Window or Johnny's Nightshirt. Straight five-card draw. Nothing wild." He puffed some more and was about to deal the first hand when he stopped and looked at Mrs. Zimmermann with a mischievous smile.

"Oh, by the way," he said, "you might bring Lewis a glass of iced tea, and get me a refill. No sugar. And bring out another plate of chocolate-chip cookies."

Mrs. Zimmermann stood up and clasped her hands subserviently in front of her. "How would you like your cookies, sir? Stuffed down your throat one by one, or crumbled up and sifted into your shirt collar?"

Jonathan stuck out his tongue at her. "Ignore her, Lewis. She thinks she's smart because she's got more college degrees than I have."

"I would be smarter than you in any case, Weird Beard. Excuse me, folks. I'll be back in a minute." She turned and walked to the kitchen.

Jonathan dealt a practice hand while she was gone. When Lewis picked his cards up, he noticed that they were old and worn. Most of the corners were missing.

But on each faded blue back was a round golden seal with an Aladdin's lamp in the middle. Above and below the seal were the words:

CAPHARNAUM COUNTY

MAGICIANS SOCIETY

Mrs. Zimmermann returned with the cookies and iced tea, and the game began in earnest. Jonathan gathered up the cards and cut them together with a very professional *zzzzzit!* He shuffled and started to deal. Lewis sipped his iced tea and felt very comfortable, very at home.

They played until midnight, by which time Lewis had red and black spots in front of his eyes. Pipe smoke hung in layers over the table and rose in a column from the shade of the floor lamp. It made the lamp seem magic, like the one on the playing cards. And there was something else magic about the game. Lewis won. He won a lot. Usually he had rotten luck, but in this game he got straight flushes, royal flushes, four of a kind. Not all of the time, but enough to keep winning steadily.

Maybe it was because Jonathan was such a lousy poker player. What Mrs. Zimmermann had said was certainly true. Whenever Jonathan had a good hand, he snortled and chortled and blew smoke out of both corners of his mouth. When he had a bad hand, he sulked and chewed his pipestem impatiently. Mrs. Zimmermann was a crafty player who could bluff you under the table with a pair of deuces, but that night she just wasn't getting the cards. Maybe that's why Lewis was winning. Maybe. But he had his doubts.

For one thing, he could have sworn that once or twice when he was reaching out to turn over a card that had been dealt to him, the card had changed. It had changed —just like that—while he was picking it up. This never happened when Lewis was dealing, but it did happen when Jonathan or Mrs. Zimmermann was dealing. And more than once he had been about to throw in a hand when, after a second look, he discovered that the hand was a good one. It was odd.

The mantel clock cleared its throat with a *whirr* and started to chime midnight.

Lewis shot a quick glance at Uncle Jonathan, who was sitting there perfectly composed, puffing his pipe. Or was he composed? He seemed to be listening for something.

The other clocks all over the house joined in. Lewis sat entranced, listening to high-pitched dings, tinny whangs, melodious electric doorbell sounds, cuckoos from cuckoo clocks, and deep sinister Chinese gongs roaring *bwaoww! bwaoww!* These and many other clock sounds echoed through the house. Now and then during this concert Lewis looked at Jonathan. Jonathan did not look back. He was staring at the wall, and his eyes had that glazed look again. Mrs. Zimmermann sat through the whole thing with her eyes fixed on the tablecloth.

The last clock to strike was the grandfather clock in the study. It made a noise like a steamer trunk full of tin plates falling slowly and solemnly down a flight of stairs. When it stopped striking, Jonathan looked up.

"Hm. Yes. Where were we? Well, Lewis, it's midnight, isn't it? Game's over. Time for bed."

Jonathan cleared the table briskly. He gathered up the playing cards, stacked them, and put a rubber band around them. Snap! Then he reached under the table and came up with a red tin candy box with a picture of the New Zebedee County Courthouse on the lid. He scraped the clattering coins into the box, snapped the lid shut, pushed back his chair, rapped out his pipe into a saucer, and folded his hands in his lap.

"Well! And what do you think of 100 High Street, Lewis?"

"I think it's wonderful, Uncle Jonathan. I like the house, and I like the town, and I like you two an awful lot."

Lewis wasn't lying. In spite of Jonathan's strange behavior and the eavesdropping habits of Mrs. Zimmermann, he had had a very good time during his first evening in New Zebedee. In fact, for most of the evening, he had had a great deal of trouble keeping himself from jumping up and down in his seat. He had been told that it was a bad thing to do in company.

Jonathan took Lewis's suitcase upstairs, and Lewis got his first look at his new room. There was a tall black bed with battlements at the top of the headboard and foot-board. In the corner was a black mirror that matched the bed, and near it was a black marble fireplace with a coffin-like black clock on its mantelpiece. Up against one wall was a tall glazed bookcase full of old books, and on top of the bookcase was a vase with cattails in it. In the middle of the floor was a large hooked rug. The pattern reminded Lewis of a map of the United States—a map of the U.S. done by a crazy person. Many children might have been put off by the dark woodwork of the old room, but Lewis loved it. He imagined that this was the sort of room Sherlock Holmes would have slept in.

Lewis got into his pajamas, put on his bathrobe and slippers, and shuffled down the hall to the bathroom. When he got back, he found that Jonathan had just finished building a fire in his fireplace.

Jonathan got up and brushed twigs off his vest. "Well, Lewis, there you are! Need anything else?"

"Gee, no, I guess not, Uncle Jonathan. This is a great room. I've always wanted a room with a fireplace in it."

Jonathan smiled. He went over to the bedside table and turned on the reading lamp. "Read as long as you like tonight, Lewis. Remember, school doesn't start for another three weeks."

"I don't know if I'll read much after all the poker playing," said Lewis, yawning. "But thanks anyway. Good night, Uncle Jonathan."

"Good night, Lewis."

Jonathan started to close the door, but he stopped. "Oh, by the way, Lewis. I hope all these clocks don't keep you awake. They're kind of noisy, but . . . well, I like them. Good night." He closed the door.

Lewis stood there with a puzzled frown on his face. There was something going on in this house that he couldn't quite get hold of. He thought of Jonathan standing paralyzed while the clock in the church steeple tolled; he thought of Mrs. Zimmermann listening at the wall. It was strange.

Oh, well, he thought, shrugging his shoulders, people are funny sometimes. Lewis climbed into bed and turned off the light. A few minutes later he turned it back on. He realized that he was still tense, excited, and wide awake.

He climbed out of bed and walked over to the shaky-looking bamboo bookcase that stood by the closet door. What a lot of old dusty books! He pulled one out and wiped the dust off with his sleeve. The faded gilt letters on the black buckram spine said:

John L.
Stoddard's
Lectures

VOL. IX
Scotland
England
London

Lewis opened the book and flipped through the slick glossy pages. He held the book up to his nose. It smelled like Old Spice talcum powder. Books that smelled that way were usually fun to read. He threw the book onto his bed and went to his suitcase. After rummaging about for a while, he came up with a long, narrow box of chocolate-covered mints. He loved to eat candy while he read, and lots of his favorite books at home had brown smudges on the corners of the pages.

A few minutes later Lewis was sitting up in bed with his pillows propped behind him. He was reading about how the Scotch nobles had murdered poor Rizzio right in front of Mary, Queen of Scots. Stoddard compared Rizzio to a purple-velvet plum spurting plum juice in all directions. The nobles dragged the poor man, kicking and screaming, into the hallway, where they stabbed him some more. Fifty-six times, said Stoddard, though he didn't say who counted the stabs. Lewis flipped the page and bit into a peppermint patty. Now Stoddard was talking about the permanence of bloodstains and wondering whether or not the stain on the hall floor in Holyrood really was Rizzio's blood or not. Lewis began to yawn. He turned off the light and went to sleep.

But he was awakened—quite suddenly—a little while later. He had been dreaming that he was being chased by the Queen of Spades. Now he sat up, wide awake. He was scared, and he didn't know why.

Creak, creak. Someone was tiptoeing down the hall.

Lewis sat still and listened. Now the sound was outside his door. Now it was going away down the hall. *Creak, creak, creak*.

Lewis slid out of bed. As slowly and carefully as he could, he tiptoed to the door. He opened it, just as slowly and carefully. He didn't open it far. Just a crack. He looked out.

The hall was dark, except for a glimmering gray window down at the far end. But Lewis could hear someone moving. And now he saw the faint, pale circle of a flashlight beam moving over the wallpaper. Frightened, Lewis pulled the door shut and then opened it just a crack. The flashlight beam had stopped. Now the figure with the flashlight brought his fist down on the wall—hard. Lewis heard little clots of plaster falling down into the space between the walls. The figure pounded again, and again. Lewis stared and opened the door wider.

Now the shadowy intruder stepped back, and Lewis saw a bulky shadow against the hall window. A bulky, bearded shadow with a pipe in its mouth. Jonathan!

Lewis closed the door as softly as he could and leaned against it, shaking. He hoped Jonathan hadn't seen him. A horrible thought came into his mind. Was Jonathan crazy?

Lewis went to the wing chair by the fire and sat down. He watched the black honeycombs as they crumbled into deep red wells. *What if Jonathan were crazy?* His parents had always warned him against crazy people, the type that lured you into their cars and offered you candy with glue in it. Or was it glue? He couldn't remember. But Jonathan didn't really seem like *that* kind of person. Or the kind that sneaked into your room at night and stabbed you to death. Lewis sighed. He would just have to wait and see what happened.

He went back to bed and had a dream in which he and Jonathan were running round and round the block that had the church on it: the church with the monster-faced steeple. All the houses on the block were lit up, but they couldn't go into any of them to hide. Something tall and dark and shapeless was following them. Finally they stopped in front of the church, and the tower began to sway as if it were made of rubber. The howling face got closer and closer . . . and then the dream changed. Lewis was sitting in a room full of glittering coins. He let them run clinking through his fingers until morning came.

CHAPTER TWO

Lewis woke up the next day with confused memories of the previous night running around in his head. In general, his impression was a happy one, despite the dark things that lurked in the corners of the picture.

He got dressed, went downstairs, and found Jonathan and Mrs. Zimmermann at breakfast. It seemed that Mrs. Zimmermann always came over to cook Jonathan's breakfast because Jonathan was such a terrible cook. Well, that was fine with Lewis. He sat down to pancakes and sausages, and before long he was figuring out how best to use the three weeks of freedom that were left before school began.

Lewis soon found out that three weeks was not nearly

enough time for exploring the town of New Zebedee and the house at 100 High Street. In three weeks he barely got started.

To begin with, the town was marvelous. It was the sort of place he had always wanted to live in. Lewis's old hometown in Wisconsin looked as if it had been built yesterday; all the houses were the same size, and the main street was just a row of bars and gas stations. New Zebedee was different. It was full of tall, elaborately decorated old houses. Even the ordinary white-frame houses had things that made them seem different—a stained-glass window or a bouquet of iron flowers on top of a cupola. And so many of the houses seemed to be hiding secrets.

Jonathan took Lewis for some walks around the town, but more often he just let Lewis find out things for himself. Sometimes Lewis just walked up and down Main Street and stared at the high, elaborate, false fronts of the stores. One of the stores had an abandoned opera house in its upper stories. Jonathan said that the old scenery was still up there, leaning against cases of Mounds bars and five-cent writing tablets. At one end of Main Street was the Civil War Monument, a fantastic stone object shaped like an artist's easel. Each of the joints and corners of the easel had a soldier or sailor standing on it, threatening the rebel army with a musket or a sword or a cannon swabber or a harpoon. The flat part of the easel was covered with the names of Capharnaum County residents who had died in the Civil War. There was a small stone arch near the monument, and it was called the Civil War Monument Annex, because it contained the names that the carvers hadn't been able to get on the big monument. Jonathan's grandfather had fought in the war with the Fifth Michigan Fire Zouave Lancers, and Jonathan was full of stories about the old man's exploits.

As for the house at 100 High Street, it was every bit as wonderful as the town, besides being strange and more than a little bit scary. There were lots of rooms to explore: third-best upstairs front parlors and second-best back bedrooms; linen closets and playrooms and just plain rooms. Some of these were empty and full of dust, but there were others that were crammed with antique furniture. There were marble-topped tables galore, and upholstered chairs on squeaky casters, and doilies pinned to the backs of the chairs, and stuffed partridges under glass bell jars. Each room had its own fireplace made of marble that looked—depending on the room—like blue cheese or fudge-ripple ice cream or green hand soap or milk chocolate.

One afternoon Lewis was walking down the back staircase in the south wing of the mansion, when he came to a stained-glass window on a landing. There were quite a few stained-glass windows in the house. Lewis found them on back staircases like this one, or in unused bathrooms or at the ends of hallways. Sometimes he even found them set in the ceiling. He had seen this one before, or rather, he had seen another window where this one was now. That was why he stopped and stared.

He remembered the other window very well. It had been a big oval window that showed a red tomato sun setting into a blue sea the color of old medicine bottles. The oval frame was still there, but in it Lewis found a window that showed a man fleeing from a forest. The forest was plum colored, and the grass under the man's feet was bright green. The sky in the picture was a squirming, oily, brownish-red. It reminded Lewis of furniture polish.

What had happened to the other window? Did Jonathan go around changing them during the night? It was pretty strange.

Another thing that was strange was the coat rack in the front hall. At first Lewis had thought that it was just an ordinary coat rack. It stood about six feet high, and it had a little round mirror on the front. There were pegs for coats and hats, and there was a little wooden compartment in the front for rubbers. It looked very ordinary. But one day when Lewis was hanging up his raincoat, he looked at the mirror and saw a Mayan step pyramid in a steaming green jungle. He knew that the pyramid was Mayan because he had a picture of it among his Viewmaster slides. Only this scene was not fake three dimensional, the way the slides were. It looked as if you could reach through the mirror and touch the vines. As

Lewis watched, a brilliant red bird with a long tail flew from one tree to another. Waves of heat made the pyramid ripple. Lewis blinked and stared again. He was looking at the reflection of the rainy gray window behind him.

Lewis thought a lot about the stained-glass windows and the coat rack. Were they magic? He believed in magic, even though he had been taught not to. His father had spent one whole afternoon explaining to Lewis that ghosts were caused by X rays bouncing off distant planets. But Lewis was a stubborn boy, and besides, hadn't he seen the Aladdin's lamp on the back of Jonathan's playing cards, and the words *Capharnaum County Magicians Society?* He was convinced that magic was at the bottom of this mystery.

Lewis was also convinced that he would have to solve another mystery before he could tackle the problem of the coat rack and the stained-glass windows. He would have to find out why Jonathan prowled the house every night with a flashlight in his hand.

Lewis had discovered that the strange incident on his first night in New Zebedee was part of a regular pattern. Every night after twelve, Jonathan was out there searching. What he was searching for, Lewis couldn't say.

Again and again, as on that first night, he had heard the floor boards creak outside his door. Again and again he had heard Jonathan tiptoeing stealthily down the hall, entering rooms, closing doors. He heard him overhead on the third floor, where Jonathan hardly ever went during the day. Then he would be back downstairs, poking around, stumbling into furniture. Maybe he was scared of burglars. Maybe so, but then why did he pound on the wall? Burglars seldom got into walls.

Lewis had to find out what was going on. And so, one night a little after twelve, Lewis lowered himself silently from his bed to the cold floor boards. As stealthily as he could, he tiptoed across the room, but the warped boards complained under his feet. By the time he got to the door, he was thoroughly shaken. He wiped his hands on his robe several times and turned the knob. He took a deep breath, let it out, and stepped out into the dark hallway.

Lewis clamped his hand over his mouth. He had stepped on the protruding head of a nail. It didn't really hurt much, but Lewis was scared of tetanus. When his panic had died down, he took another step. He began to edge his way down the hall.

But Lewis was no better at stealthy creeping than you might think and, by the time he had bumped his head against a heavy, gilt picture frame for about the third time, Jonathan called to him from one of the distant rooms.

"Oh, for heaven's sake, Lewis! Stop playing Sherlock Holmes! You make a better Dr. Watson. Come on and join me. I'm in the bedroom with the green fireplace."

Lewis was glad that his red face didn't shine in the dark. Well, at least Jonathan wasn't mad.

Lewis picked his way down the hall until he found an open door. There was Jonathan, standing in the dark with a flashlight in his hand. He was playing the light over the mantel clock, a boxy black affair with gold handles on the sides, like a coffin.

"Evening, Lewis. Or morning, as the case may be. Would you care to join me on my rounds?"

Jonathan's voice sounded tight and nervous. Lewis hesitated a moment and then he plunged in. "Uncle Jonathan, what are you doing?"

"Stopping the clocks. During the day it's nice to have clocks ticking all over the house, but at night it keeps me awake. You know how it is, Lewis, with faucets and . . . and the like."

Still chattering nervously, Jonathan turned the clock around, reached into the back of it, and halted the stubby pendulum. Then he motioned for Lewis to follow him and, waving the flashlight a little too cheerfully, walked on to the next room. Lewis followed, but he was puzzled. "Uncle Jonathan, why don't you turn the room lights on?"

His uncle was silent for a minute. Then he said, in that same nervous voice, "Oh, well, you know how it is, Lewis. If I were to go from one room to another snapping lights on and off, what would the neighbors think? And what about the electric bill? Do you know that you get billed for an hour's worth of electricity every time you snap the lights on and off?"

This explanation did not sound convincing to Lewis. In the first place, Uncle Jonathan had never before given any sign that he cared what the neighbors thought about anything he did. If he wanted to sit in the glider under the chestnut tree and play a saxophone at 3 A.M. he was likely to do just that. In the second place, Jonathan had more than once left the floor lamp in his study burning all night. He was a careless man, and not the sort who worried about big electric bills. It was true that Lewis had only known his uncle for three weeks, but he felt that he already had a pretty good idea of what Jonathan was like.

On the other hand, he couldn't very well say, "Uncle Jonathan, you're lying through your teeth!" so he silently followed his uncle to the next room, the second-best upstairs bathroom. It had a fireplace too—a white tile one—and there was a small, white plastic clock buzzing on the mantel. Jonathan unplugged it without saying anything and went on to the next room, where he stopped a cherrywood clock with a pendulum that used three columns of mercury as a weight. And then on to the next room.

The last clock to be silenced was the grandfather clock in the study. Jonathan's study had a very high ceiling, and all the walls were lined with books. There was a fat, slouchy, brown-leather easy chair that hissed when you sat down in it and, of course, there was a fireplace, and there was still a fire burning in it. Over in a corner by the sliding doors that opened into the dining room stood the tall gloomy clock. The brass disk on the pendulum flashed dimly in the light of the dying fire. Jonathan reached inside and grabbed the long black rod. The clock stopped.

Now that their strange tour was over, Jonathan lapsed into silence. He seemed to be thinking. He walked over to the fireplace, stirred up the fire, and put on another log. He threw himself down into the leather chair and waved his arm at the green easy chair on the other side of the fireplace.

"Have a seat, Lewis. I'd like to have a talk with you."

Lewis wondered if he was going to get bawled out for sneaking up on his uncle. It didn't seem likely. Jonathan looked and sounded friendly, though his voice was still a little edgy. Lewis sat down and watched as Jonathan lit up his hookah. Lewis always liked to watch him do this. The hookah was shaped like a Spanish galleon, and the crow's nest on the mainmast was the bowl. The body of the ship was full of water for cooling the smoke, and up on the bow stood the tiny ceramic figure of a boatswain with his pipe to his lips. A long hose was plugged into the ship's stern, and there was a black rubber mouthpiece on the end. When you blew into the hose, the burning tobacco in the crow's nest sent up a long column of smoke, and the boatswain went *fweee!* on his little pipe. Sometimes, when Jonathan made a mistake and filled the boat too full of water, the boatswain went *blp!* and blew bubbles.

When Jonathan had the pipe going good, he drew in a big mouthful of smoke, let it out slowly, and said, "Lewis, I think it would be better for you to be scared than it would be for you to think of your uncle as a crabby old lunatic."

"I don't think you're crabby," said Lewis.

Jonathan laughed. "But you *do* think I'm off my rocker. Well, after tonight I wouldn't blame you."

Lewis blushed. "No, Uncle Jonathan! I never meant that! You know I don't think . . ."

Jonathan smiled. "Yes, of course, I know. But all the same, I think it would be better if you knew something about this clock business. I can't tell you all about it because I don't know all about it. In fact, there are times when I think I don't know much about it at all. But I'll tell you what I know."

He crossed his legs, sat back, and puffed some more at his pipe. Lewis sat forward in the big green chair. He kept clasping and unclasping his hands and he stared hard at Jonathan. After a brief dramatic pause and a particularly long drag at the galleon-hookah, Jonathan began.

"I haven't lived in this house always, Lewis. In fact, I only moved here five years ago. I used to live down on Spruce Street, near the waterworks. But when the old owner died, and the place was put up for sale cheap, and it meant a chance to live next door to my best friend, Mrs. Zimmermann—"

"Who was the old owner?" asked Lewis, interrupting.

"I was going to get around to that. His name was Isaac Izard. Initials I.I., like a Roman numeral II. You'll find his double *I* carved or painted or stamped on all sorts of things all over this house: the wainscoting, the floorboards, the insides of cupboards, the fuse box, the mantelpieces—everywhere. You'll even find a Roman numeral II worked into the tracery on the wallpaper in the upstairs front hallway." Jonathan paused for a second and looked thoughtful. "Have to get that paper replaced some day . . . oh, well, back to what I was saying. Old Isaac Izard—his name is odd, isn't it? Mrs. Zimmermann thinks that it comes from *izzard*, which in some parts of England is the word for *zed*, which is the word the English use to identify the letter Z. I go along with Mrs. Zimmermann's theory because I can't think of a better one. And besides, she is a Z-lady, so she should know. But, as I was saying, and I will get around to saying something *sometime*, Lewis . . ." He puffed on his pipe some more and wriggled around in the chair to get comfortable. "As I was saying, old Isaac was a warlock."

"What's that?"

Uncle Jonathan looked very serious. "It's the word for a male witch."

Lewis shuddered. Then, out of nowhere, a strange

/ 33 /

thought came to him. "Are you one too?" he asked in a tiny, frightened voice.

Jonathan looked at him with a strange smile. "Would it scare you if I said I was?"

"No. I like you an awful lot and you can be a warlock if you want to be one, I guess. You wouldn't be a bad one, I know."

"That depends on how you mean 'bad,' " said Jonathan, chuckling. "If you mean that I wouldn't be an evil one, you're right. If you mean that I wouldn't be too bad at wizarding . . . well, I don't know. I'm pretty much of a parlor magician, though I have a few tricks that go beyond rabbits and playing cards."

"Like stained-glass windows and coat racks?" said Lewis, grinning.

"Yes. Exactly like those. And just to make you *perfectly* secure, let me inform you that Mrs. Zimmermann is also a wizard, though in her case the term should be witch."

"Couldn't you find a better name?" asked Lewis timidly.

"Well, she prefers 'maga' or 'enchantrix,' but I can't use such words without breaking up, so she's old witch Florence to me. She's really a much more serious wizard than I am. Got her D.Mag.A.—that's *Doctor Magicorum Artium*—from the University of Göttingen in Germany in 1922. I just have an A.B. from Michigan Agricultural College."

"What in?" asked Lewis, as if he were interviewing Jonathan for a job. Actually he was interested in Jonathan's college work. Both of Lewis's parents had gone to college, and they always talked a lot about their college work.

"What in?" said Jonathan, blushing. "What in? Why, Agricultural Science. Animal Husbandry and all that. I was going to be a farmer till my grandpa died and left me a pile of money. But back to Isaac Izard. You're still interested, aren't you?"

"Oh, yes! Of course! Please tell me. I want to know."

"Isaac, as I say, was a wizard. He fooled around with black magic, the worst kind of thing a wizard can do. I can't tell you about anything bad that I absolutely know he did—for sure—but if one wizard can judge another, I'd say he was an evil one. A very evil one. Mrs. Zimmermann thinks so too. She lived next door to him for years, remember. You'll have to ask her about him yourself, of course, but there were many evenings when she and I would stand in her back yard and look up and see old Isaac's evil face in the window of the cupola on top of the house. He'd be holding an oil lamp and just staring out at the night. Mrs. Zimmermann claims that he would sit for hours in the cupola during the day. He seemed to be taking notes."

"Gee, that *is* weird. What was he taking notes for?"

"Lord only knows, Lewis. But I'm sure it wasn't anything good. At any rate, to get on with my story. . . . It

/ 35 /

must be getting pretty late by now, but without the clocks I have no idea what time it is. Where was I? Oh, yes. Old Isaac died during a wild thunderstorm, one of the worst in the history of Capharnaum County. You can look it up in the New Zebedee *Chronicle* if you want to: roofs blown off barns, trees uprooted, and a bolt of lightning melted the iron doors on the tomb Isaac is buried in now. I'll have to show you that tomb some day. Ugly old dump—one of those little stone houses for the respectable dead. There are several of them up in our cemetery, some of them really fancy. This one was built by Isaac's family in the 1850's, but it was never used till they put his wife in there. She died before he did."

"What was she like?"

"Pretty strange, as you'd have to be to choose Isaac Izard for a husband. I don't remember anything about her but her eyeglasses."

Lewis stared. "Her eyeglasses?"

"Yes. I passed her once on the street and she turned and looked at me. It might have been the way the sun caught her spectacles, but I remember two freezing circles of gray light burning into me. I turned away and closed my eyes, but those two cold spots stayed there. I had nightmares for a week after that."

"How did she die?" Lewis imagined Mrs. Izard falling from a cliff during a hurricane, or flinging herself from the cupola of the house.

"How? Quietly and mysteriously. No funeral. Some

strange-looking people from out of town came and helped Isaac bury her. After that, he went into seclusion. Further seclusion, that is. He and she had always been hermits, but after her death he really shut himself up. Built a big high board fence between this house and Mrs. Zimmermann's. I had it torn down as soon as I moved in." He smiled contentedly. Lewis felt that his Uncle Jonathan was happy living at 100 High Street, despite the fact that old Isaac Izard had made the place his castle.

"Is that all there is to the story?" asked Lewis cautiously.

"Oh, my, no. We're just getting to the good part. Look, here I am selfishly puffing away at this boat, and you have nothing. Let's go out to the kitchen and get a couple of glasses of milk and some chocolate-chip cookies. Okay?"

"Sure!" said Lewis, who liked chocolate-chip cookies even more than he liked Welch's Fudge Bars.

In a few minutes they were back in the study, sitting by the quietly crackling fire and munching cookies. Suddenly a book fell out of the bookcase. *Flop*. Two more fell out. *Flop. Flop*. Lewis stared at the black gap in the row of books. A long, withered, bony hand appeared. It seemed to be groping for something.

Lewis sat rigid with terror, but Jonathan merely smiled. "A little to your left, my dear. That's it. Now you've got it."

A latch clicked and a large section of the built-in bookcase swung outwards. More books fell to the floor. And there stood Mrs. Zimmermann, with a strand of cobweb hanging from her left eyeglass. Her sleeve was covered with whitish dust.

"Fine way to build a secret panel," she grumbled. "With the latch on the room side instead of on the passage side."

"It adds to the mystery, Doll Face. As you might have guessed, Lewis, this house has a secret passageway. You enter it through the china cupboard in the kitchen. Come on in, Florence. I was just going to tell Lewis about the clock in the walls."

Mrs. Zimmermann gave him a look as if to say, "Do you think that's a wise thing to do?" But she shrugged and helped herself to the cookies and milk.

"Good cookies," she said, munching. "Very good."

"She always says that because she makes them," explained Jonathan, helping himself to two more. "And now that everyone's mouth is stuffed, including mine, I guess I'll go on. Where were we? Oh, yes. Well, I had no sooner moved in here than I felt that something was wrong. The house had a kind of listening stillness. And then I heard it."

"Heard what?" This was Lewis, who had worked himself to the edge of his chair. He had even stopped eating his cookie.

"The clock. You know how you can be in a room with

a clock ticking, and you won't notice it for a long time. Then, when things are very, very quiet and you aren't thinking about anything in particular—there it is!"

Lewis jumped up and looked around wildly. "Where?"

Jonathan laughed. "No, no, no. I didn't mean to frighten you like that. I mean I heard it for the first time in this room. It was ticking away in the walls. You can go over to that wall and listen for it, if you like."

Lewis got up and walked over to the book-lined wall. He put his ear to a row of black leather volumes and listened. His eyes opened wide.

"It *is* there, Uncle Jonathan! It is!" He was excited by the discovery, but then his face changed. He looked afraid. "What is it for, Uncle Jonathan? What does it do?"

"I haven't the faintest idea," said Jonathan, "though I know that I want to blot it out. That's why I have all these stupid clocks. I didn't used to be so fond of incessant ticking and sudden, loud, hell raising every hour on the hour. But I prefer my clocks to his."

Jonathan's face had turned grim. He shook his head, smiled a little half-hearted smile, and went on. "You may be wondering why I don't just tear down the wall and rip out the clock. Well, it wouldn't do any good. It sounds like it's behind every wall: up in the attic, down in the cellar, in the closets and storerooms and parlors. And sometimes it seems to be slowing down. I keep hoping it will stop. But then it picks up and keeps going.

I don't know what to do." There was a note of real despair in his voice. For a minute Lewis thought his uncle would cry. Then Mrs. Zimmermann broke in.

"I'll tell you one thing you ought *not* to do, Jonathan Barnavelt. You oughtn't to frighten Lewis with something you don't know anything about. After all, the ticking may be some leftover magic from the old coot's experiments. Or death-watch beetles. Or an illusion of some kind, like in houses that have whispering galleries. I get a funny kind of hum in my head now and then. It goes *dooooo* for a while and then it goes away."

Jonathan looked irritated. "Oh, Florence, there's no need to kid around. You don't think it's something harmless and neither do I. I wouldn't have told Lewis just to frighten him. But I thought it would be better for him to know about the clock than to think that his uncle was getting ready for the loony bin. You see, he caught me making my nightly rounds."

"Well," said Mrs. Zimmermann, "I don't know about the loony bin, but Uncle Jonathan had better be getting ready for beddy-by if he's going to take us on a picnic tomorrow." She reached into the folds of her dress and pulled out a silver watch on a long chain. She popped the lid open and announced that it was three A.M.

Jonathan looked up with surprise. "It is? Good grief, I had no idea——"

"Please, Uncle Jonathan," said Lewis, interrupting. "Can you tell me one thing more?"

"Sure, Lewis. What is it?"

Lewis looked fidgety and embarrassed. "Well . . . if the clocks are supposed to drown out the noise of the clock in the walls, why do you stop them at night?"

Jonathan sighed. "I don't stop them every night. Some nights I just walk around checking all the rooms. It makes me feel secure, somehow. I can't explain it. But some nights, like this one, I get the urge to stop all the blasted everlasting ticking. I get the feeling that if I were to make the house quiet—perfectly quiet—then maybe I could hear the real clock, the magic one, ticking behind one particular wall, or in some cubbyhole. But it never works, and I always feel half crazy for trying."

Lewis still looked puzzled. "If it's a magic clock," he said slowly, "then wouldn't it be invisible? I mean, wouldn't it be something you couldn't actually put your hands on?"

Jonathan shook his head. "Not really, Lewis. Most magic is accomplished with solid everyday objects. Objects that have had spells said over them. One witch I knew tried to obliterate her enemy by leaving a photo of him under the running water of her gutterspout. Her reasoning was that he would die when the face on the picture was wiped out. It's a common method. No, Lewis. This is a clock as real as grandpa over there. Only it's enchanted. But what it is enchanted to do I don't for the life of me know."

"Well, *I* know something, Weird Beard," said Mrs.

Zimmermann, dangling her watch like a pendulum before Jonathan's eyes, "I know that if we don't catch just a little, teeny bit of shut-eye, we're all going to be wearing our crabby caps in the morning. Lewis, off to bed. Jonathan, same with you. I'll rinse the cookie plates and put away the milk."

Later, up in his room, Lewis stood in the middle of the floor staring at a patch of flowered wallpaper near the fireplace. He walked quickly over to the wall and put his ear to it. Yes, the ticking was here too. He walked across the room and listened to another wall. More of the same.

Lewis walked back to the center of the room and then, abruptly, he began to pace. He paced in quick strides with his hands behind his back, the way he had seen his father do when he was upset. He paced and tried to think logically. But logic wasn't much help where the clock in the walls was concerned, so at last Lewis gave it up. He jumped into bed and went to sleep.

CHAPTER THREE

On the first Monday after Labor Day, Lewis started going to school in New Zebedee and, before long, he had forgotten all about the mysterious clock in the walls. He had troubles enough of his own.

They weren't new troubles. They were the troubles that a fat boy who can't play baseball carries around with him from place to place. Lewis had always been overweight. He couldn't remember a time when he hadn't been. All his life—all ten years of it—he had been listening to children who chanted:

> Fatty, fatty, two by four
> Can't get through the kitchen door.

Sometimes he wanted to beat up the kids who made fun of him, but he couldn't box and he wasn't very strong. That was another problem. But the worst problem of all was the baseball problem. Lewis still spun all the way around when he swung at a ball, and he threw his bat. At first he tried to excuse himself by saying, "Watch out, I'm gonna throw the bat!" But the other kids said, "Look, you throw the bat and we're gonna beat you up. You hang onto it when you swing or you can't play."

That is what they said when they let him play, which was not very often. Most of the time when he lined up to be chosen he was the last one left, and the captain of the side that was supposed to take him usually said, "Why do we hafta take *him?* He can't field, he can't hit, he can't pitch. He can't even run. Come on, we'll play one man short."

What they said about Lewis was true. Sometimes a new boy or a kind boy would get to be captain, and he would choose Lewis for his team. But when Lewis came to bat, he usually struck out. If he hit the ball, it popped up and the pitcher caught it. Or he might ground out to first base. When his team was out in the field, the boys made Lewis play right field, because not many balls got hit out that way. But when one did, Lewis always dropped it, unless it hit him on the head. He would stagger back and forth as he tried to keep track of the ball that hung there, high over his head, but he always got dizzy and covered his face with his glove and screamed "No! No!" as the ball came down. After a while even the kind boys turned him down.

One afternoon, when the usual routine had been gone through, and Lewis had run off the field sobbing because they would not let him play, he found himself standing at home plate on a baseball diamond that wasn't being used that day. At his feet was a bat, a thick old club with a split handle that had been wrapped up with black friction tape. There was a softball nearby, or what was left of one: a black, sticky, egg-shaped lump covered with string. Lewis picked up the ball and bat. He threw the ball into the air and swung at it. He missed. He picked the ball up and tried again. Again he missed. He was about to try for the third time when someone said, "You're doin' it all wrong."

Lewis turned and saw a skinny boy about his own age squatting next to the bicycle rack. There was a big fluff of brick-red hair on top of the boy's head, and his right arm was in a sling. The boy was Tarby.

Everybody in the school knew who Tarby was. Even Lewis knew, and he had only been in New Zebedee for a couple of months. Probably everyone in New Zebedee and most of the people in Capharnaum County knew who Tarby was. At least, that was the impression that Lewis got. Tarby was the most popular boy in the school. He was a daredevil, the kind of boy who rode his bicycle through bonfires and hung by his knees from the limbs of trees. All the girls liked him, and he was the big home-run hitter in the softball games. He got chosen first so often that most of the time the boys made him a captain, just to avoid all the fighting over who got to have Tarby on their team. But here he was with his arm in a sling, watching Lewis as he tried to hit the ball.

"I said, you're doing it all wrong. You're supposed to keep your feet planted flat. Then you swing from the hips. Here. Let me show you."

Tarby scrambled to his feet and walked over to where Lewis was standing. He grabbed the bat and hefted it in one hand, choking up on it a bit.

"Okay," he said, "get out there and pitch. Just lob it up here."

Lewis had never seen anyone trying to hit a ball with the bat held in only one hand. He was afraid that Tarby would miss and get mad and go home. With a nervous grin on his face, Lewis lobbed the ball toward the plate. Tarby swung and the bat connected. *Clack!* It struck the ball with that rickety hollow sound that split bats have. The ball shot on a line toward center field. It would have been a clean single.

"See? And that's just with one arm. You ought to be able to do that well with two. C'mon. I'll pitch."

Lewis walked in from the pitcher's mound and took the bat from Tarby's hand.

"I didn't know your arm was broken," said Lewis shyly. "How'd you do it?"

"Fell out of a tree. I was hanging by my knees. Upside down, like in the monkey house. It's okay. It'll heal up."

Tarby walked out to the mound. Lewis pounded his bat on the plate and waved it the way he had seen George Kell do in Briggs Stadium in Detroit. But when Tarby threw the ball, Lewis missed as usual.

Every day for the next two weeks Tarby met Lewis after school, and they practiced batting. Slowly, gradually, Lewis's swing got better. He even managed to hit a few line drives. But something even more important was happening. Lewis and Tarby were getting to be friends. Tarby liked Lewis's jokes, and Lewis found out that Tarby hated some of the kids that he hated. Lewis liked Tarby's imitation of Mrs. Fondrighter, a mean teacher at school. Mrs. Fondrighter always called her husband "Jerrold," which was a funny thing to do. Tarby made a loop in the end of a green twig and pretended it was an eyeglass on a stick. Then he would stare through the loop at Lewis and say, in a high voice, "How *deah* you say such things to me, Jer-*rold!*"

Then Lewis and Tarby would sit around planning how they were going to take care of Carol Kay Laberdeen, a snotty girl in the sixth grade who got away with murder because her father was on the school board. It was usually dark by the time Lewis and Tarby said goodby to each other by the mailbox at the bottom of High Street.

One afternoon early in October, Lewis and Tarby

were out at the athletic field playing flies and grounders. Lewis had gotten good enough so that he could hit Tarby some pretty long fly balls. Tarby's arm was still in a cast, but he picked off the line drives and caught the pop flies as easily as if he had had two hands.

Lewis was out in the field. It was getting dark, and he was having trouble seeing the ball, and besides he was a little bored. He stood there thinking, or "doping off" as Tarby called it.

He wanted to do something nice for Tarby. Something nice that would really impress him and make him a stronger friend than ever. Maybe he could get Uncle Jonathan to do a magic trick for Tarby. Sure, that would do it. Lewis hesitated a minute, remembering Jonathan saying that he was only a "parlor magician." The kind that pulled rabbits out of hats and told you what card you were holding in your hand. But then he *had* said that he knew a few tricks that went beyond that. . . .

Lewis thought some more. Oh, well, Jonathan could probably do it. Anyone who could make windows change their pictures could do what Lewis had in mind. And anyway, Lewis thought that he remembered hearing Jonathan say that he had done such a thing once.

"Hey, Lewis! I hit the ball out to you about six hours ago. Did you go to sleep?"

Lewis looked up. "Huh? Oh, gee, I'm sorry, Tarby. Say, how would you like to see my uncle eclipse the moon?"

Tarby stared at him. "What did you say?"

"I said . . . oh, c'mon, Tarby, let's go home. It's too dark to see the ball. C'mon and I'll tell you all about my Uncle Jonathan. He's a real wizard."

The two boys walked back under the streetlights, playing catch as they went. Lewis tried to explain about Uncle Jonathan's magic powers, but he could see that Tarby was not convinced.

"Boy, I'll *bet* your uncle can eclipse the moon. I'll just *bet* he can. He prob'ly sits up in his room drinking beer, and then he goes out in back and stares up at the moon, and boy does it go rround . . . and . . . rraounnd." Tarby staggered out into the street and rolled his eyes.

Lewis felt like hitting him, but he knew that Tarby could beat him up, so he just said, "You wanta see him do it?"

"Yeah," said Tarby in a sneery voice. "I wanta see him do it."

"Okay," said Lewis. "I'll ask him tonight. When he's ready to do it, I'll let you know."

"Gee, I hope I won't have to wait too long," said Tarby sarcastically. "I really do want to see Old Lard Guts eclipse the moo-hoo-hoo, moo-hoo-ha . . . ."

"Stop it. Stop making fun of my uncle." Lewis's face was red, and he was almost crying.

"Make me," said Tarby.

"I can't, and you know it," said Lewis.

Tarby went on moo-hooing until they reached the

khaki-colored mailbox at the foot of High Street. This time when they split up to go home, Lewis didn't say goodby to Tarby. He didn't even wave. But by the time he was inside the gate at 100 High Street, Lewis had gotten over his mad—more or less—and so he went straight inside to see his uncle. He found Jonathan laying out a game of solitaire on the dining-room table. It was a complicated game called "Napoleon at St. Helena," and the layout covered most of the ivory-colored oilcloth pad. Jonathan looked up and smiled as Lewis walked into the room.

"Hi, Lewis! How's baseball these days?"

"Getting better, I guess. Tarby helps me a lot. Say, Uncle Jonathan, do you suppose we could do something nice for Tarby? He really is a good friend of mine."

"Sure, Lewis. We'll invite him to dinner. Is that what you mean?"

Lewis blushed and fidgeted. "Uh . . . well, yeah . . . kind of. Do you think that maybe after dinner we could . . . uh, that is, *you* could . . . eclipse the moon for him?"

Jonathan stared at him. "Did I tell you I could do *that?*"

"Yes. Remember, one night when you were bragging . . . er, talking to Mrs. Zimmermann about whether earth magic was stronger than moon magic? You said that a moon wizard could eclipse the moon any time he felt like it, and that you were a moon wizard."

Jonathan smiled and shook his head. "Did I say that? My, my, how I do run on. Let me see, I do seem to recall eclipsing the moon one night in 1932. That was during a picnic out at Wilder Creek Park. I remember the date, April 30, which is Walpurgis Night. That's the night when witches and warlocks all over the world get together for whoop-te-doos. Ours was just a convention of the Capharnaum County Magicians Society, but some of them are real wizards. At any rate, to get back to what I was saying . . ."

"Never mind," said Lewis, turning away with a pouty look on his face. "I'll tell Tarby that you can't do it."

"Oh, Lewis!" cried Jonathan, throwing the pack of cards down on the table. "You are the most easily discouraged boy I ever met. If I did it once, I can do it again. It's just that it's not a normal occurrence. And everything has to be just right. In the heavens, that is."

"Oh."

"Yes, oh. Now, as soon as I have won this silly game from myself, you and I will go to the library and consult the almanac. So be quiet for a minute."

Lewis fidgeted and clasped and unclasped his hands and stared at the light fixture until Jonathan finished his game. Then the two of them went to the library, slid back the panelled doors, and entered the marvelous room that smelled of damp paper, wood smoke, and Turkoman's Terror, Jonathan's personal tobacco blend. Jonathan moved the stepladder to the part of the wall that contained his magic books, climbed up, and pulled down a thick dusty volume labelled:

HARDESTY'S
Universal Omnium Gatherum

*Perpetual Calendar, Date Book,
Almanac, and Book of Days*

He flipped to the section on eclipses, did some rapid mental calculations, and said, "You're in luck, Lewis. 1948 is a good year for lunar eclipses. The planets will be favorable next Friday. Invite Tarby to dinner for that night. I'll be ready."

Friday night came around, and Lewis brought Tarby home for dinner. There was nothing especially magic about the meal, except that the cider jug on the table burped a lot, and that might have been because the cider was getting hard. After the dishes were cleared away, Jonathan asked Lewis and Tarby to help Mrs. Zimmermann carry some kitchen chairs out into the back yard. Then he walked out into the front hall and consulted his cane rack, a blue Willoware vase full of walking sticks of all sizes and shapes. Some had ivory or bone handles, some were tough, crooked old pieces of hickory or maplewood, and some had thin springy swords concealed inside. But only one cane was magic.

It was a long black rod of some very hard wood. At one end was a ferrule of polished brass, and at the other was a glass globe the size of a baseball. It seemed to be snowing inside the globe. Through the swirling little flakes you could see, now and then, an odd little miniature castle. The globe burned with an icy gray light. Jonathan picked up the cane, hefted it, and walked back toward the kitchen with it tucked under his arm.

Out in the back yard, the audience was ready. Mrs. Zimmermann, Lewis, and Tarby sat in straight chairs facing the birdbath. It was a chilly, clear October night. All the stars were out, and a large full moon was rising over the four elm trees at the far end of Jonathan's yard. The screen door slammed, and everyone looked up. The magician had arrived.

Without saying a word, Jonathan went around to the north side of the house. An old mossy rain barrel stood there against the sandstone wall. Jonathan looked into the barrel, breathed three times on the dark water, and with his left forefinger cut the faintly shimmering surface into four quarters. Then he leaned low over the mouth of the barrel and began whispering in a strange language. The three spectators had not left their chairs—Jonathan had told them to stay where they were—but they craned their necks around a good deal trying to figure out what the wizard was doing.

The whispering, weirdly magnified by the mouth of

the barrel, went on for some time. Lewis twisted way around in his chair, but all he could see was the dark shape of Uncle Jonathan and the faintly glowing gray globe of the magic cane. Finally Jonathan returned. In one hand he held the cane, and in the other he had a saucepan full of rain water.

"Is your uncle going to wash his hair?" whispered Tarby.

"Oh, be quiet!" hissed Lewis. "He knows what he's doing. Just you watch."

Tarby, Lewis, and Mrs. Zimmermann watched anxiously as Jonathan poured the saucepan into the birdbath. Then he went back to the rain barrel for more. *Dip. Splash.* He came back with another panful. He emptied it. And he went back for a third.

The third panful seemed to be enough. Jonathan set down the empty pan and picked up his cane, which had been leaning against the birdbath. The glass ball glowed and sent out a ray of dusty gray light. The ray rested on the surface of the water in the birdbath. Jonathan made signs over the water with the cane and started muttering again.

"Come on and look," he said, motioning to the three spectators. They got up and walked over to the birdbath. The water in the flat, shallow concrete pan had started to heave and pitch, like ocean water in a storm. Lewis was surprised to see tiny whitecaps forming. Then long rollers began to crash silently into the rim, sending pin-point flecks of foam out onto the grass. Jonathan watched for a while along with the rest. Then, suddenly, he raised the cane and cried, "Peace! Peace to the waters of the earth! Show unto us the round disk of the moon, even as she now appeareth in the heavens above!"

The water calmed down. Soon it was a flat pool again, and floating on the still black surface was the cold reflection of the full moon. Now Jonathan did something very unlikely. As the others watched, he bent over and pulled a small boulder out of the pile of rocks at the base of the birdbath. Then, lifting it high in the air, he shouted, "Stand back!" and dropped the rock. *Splash!* Water slopped everywhere, and Lewis did not get out of the way soon enough to keep from getting some on his shoes.

When the water had calmed down again, Jonathan picked up the rock and looked into the pool. There, wobbly and creased with ripples, was the moon's reflection.

"Still there?" said Jonathan, grinning. "Well, we'll just see about that!"

He reached down into the water and picked up the reflection. It might have been a trick, but the cold, icy-gray disk he held up looked like the reflection that had floated in the pool a moment before. And sure enough, when Lewis looked into the water, all he saw now was a shiny blackness.

Jonathan held up the reflection and turned it back and forth as if it were a dinner plate. The disk burned cold and bitter, and sparkled like freshly fallen snow. It hurt Lewis's eyes to stare at it for very long. Now Jonathan snapped his wrist and sent the disk flying across the yard. It sailed clear across to the dark thicket in front of the four elm trees. Then Jonathan, cane in hand, ran off after the disk. It was a long yard and, even in the moonlight, the boys and Mrs. Zimmermann could not see what he was doing down there.

Suddenly the air was filled with the inane glockling and blockling of bamboo wind chimes. There was a set of them hanging from one of the elm trees, and Jonathan had given it a good hard yank. Now he came dancing back up the yard, dueling with shadows and saying things like, "Ha! Have at you in your bladder for a blaggardly slacker! Hoo! Hunh! And the third in his bosom!"

He stopped in front of the birdbath and held the ball of the cane up under his chin so that his face looked like an actor's face when it is lit from below by footlights. Slowly he raised his right hand and pointed at the sky. "Look!" he cried.

All three of the spectators looked up. At first they saw nothing strange. Then, slowly, a black, tarry, drippy shadow oozed down over the face of the surprised moon. In no time at all the moon was dark, completely dark, blacked out, without even the faint brownish umbra that marks its place during an ordinary eclipse.

And now Uncle Jonathan's back yard came to life. It was full of strange sights and sounds. The grass glowed a phosphorescent green, and red worms wriggled through the tall blades with a hushing sound. Strange insects dropped down out of the overhanging boughs of the willow tree and started to dance on the picnic table. They waltzed and wiggled in a shaking blue light, and the music they danced to, faint though it was, sounded to Lewis like "Rugbug," the famous fox trot composed by Maxine Hollister. This was one of the tunes that Jonathan's parlor organ played.

Uncle Jonathan walked over to the tulip bed, put his ear to the ground, and listened. He motioned for the others to join him. Lewis put his ear to the damp earth, and he heard strange things. He heard the noise that earthworms make as they slowly inch along, breaking hard black clods with their blunt heads. He heard the secret inwound conversations of bulbs and roots, and the breathing of flowers. And Lewis knew strange things, without knowing how he came to know them. He knew that there was a cat named Texaco buried in the patch of ground he knelt on. Its delicate ivory skeleton was falling slowly to pieces down there, and its dank fur was shrivelled and matted and rotten. The boy who had buried the cat had buried a sand pail full of shells near it. Lewis did not know the name of the boy, or how long ago he had buried the cat and the pail, but he could see the red and blue pail clearly. Blotches of brown rust were eating up the bright designs, and the shells were covered with green mold.

After a long while, Lewis sat up and looked around. Tarby was kneeling near him, his ear to the ground and his eyes wide with wonder. But where was Uncle Jonathan? Where, for that matter, was Mrs. Zimmermann? At the far end of the yard, in the shadow of the four elm trees, Lewis thought he saw them moving around. He tapped Tarby on the shoulder, pointed, and the two boys silently got up and went to join the magicians.

When they found them, Jonathan was arguing with Mrs. Zimmermann, who argued right back, though her ear was pressed flat to the ground.

"I say it's the old storm sewer system," she muttered. "It was lost track of in 1868 because the charts got thrown out with the wastepaper."

"Well, you can think what you like, Frizzy Wig," said Jonathan as he knelt down for another listen. "*I* say it's an underground stream. Capharnaum County is full of them, and it would account for the fact that Sin-and-Flesh Creek is much bigger when it leaves New Zebedee than it is when it enters it."

"You're full of beans, Fatso," said Mrs. Zimmermann, whose ear was still pressed to the ground. "I think I know the sound of water rushing through a brick tunnel. It's all vaulty and hollow."

"Like your head?"

Lewis and Tarby pressed their ears to the ground, but

all they could hear was a sound like the one you hear when you press your ear against an inner tube that you are floating on in a lake. Lewis felt very excited. He wanted to be all over the garden at once, touching things and smelling them and listening. The magic in the back yard lasted for over an hour. Then the phosphorescence changed to plain old ordinary moonlight, and the moon floated high overhead, free from enchantments.

As they walked back into the house, Lewis asked his uncle if the police department didn't get mad when he eclipsed the moon. Jonathan chuckled and put his arm around Lewis.

"No," he said, "strangely enough they don't. I've never been quite sure why, but maybe it's because the eclipse is only visible in this yard."

"You mean it's not real?"

"Of course, it's real. You saw it, didn't you? But one of the troubles with human beings is that they can only see out of their own eyes. If I could be two people, I'd station the other me across town to see if the eclipse was operating over there."

"Why don't you ask Mrs. Zimmermann to go watch?"

"Because she'd be crabby. She always wants to be in on things. Don't you, Pruny?"

"Yes, I do. And right now I'd like to be in on some chocolate-chip cookies. Why don't you all come over to my place?"

And that is what they did. Lewis was happy to have a chance to show off Mrs. Zimmermann's house to Tarby. It was not a mansion, by any means. Just a little two-story bungalow with a screened-in front porch. But it was full of strange things, most of them purple. Mrs. Zimmermann had a thing about the color purple. Her rugs, her wallpaper, her staircase runner, her toilet paper, and her bath soap were all purple. So was the large surrealistic painting of a dragon that hung in her living room. It had been done for her specially by the French painter Odilon Redon.

As they munched their cookies and drank their milk and walked around looking at the purple things in Mrs. Zimmermann's house, Lewis noticed that Tarby wasn't saying much. When it came time for him to go, Tarby shook Jonathan's hand while staring at the carpet, and he mumbled, "Thanks for the cookies" to Mrs. Zimmermann in such a low voice that he couldn't be understood. Lewis saw Tarby to the front gate. He knew this was odd behavior for Tarby, who was usually loud and sassy-acting, even in front of grownups.

"Thanks for the magic show," said Tarby, shaking Lewis's hand and looking very serious. "It was kind of scary, but it was fun. I take back all the things I said about your uncle, I guess. Well, see you around." And with that, Tarby went trudging down the hill.

Lewis stared after him with a worried frown on his

face. He hoped that Tarby had had a good time. Most people do not like to be proven wrong, even when they enjoy themselves in the process. Tarby was a popular boy, and he was used to being right about everything. He had turned out to be wrong about Jonathan's magic powers. Now what would he do? Lewis didn't want to lose his only friend.

CHAPTER FOUR

It was the last week of October, and Tarby's arm had almost healed. Lewis saw less and less of him now. He still waited for him on the baseball diamond out behind the school, and sometimes Tarby showed up, and sometimes he didn't.

Of course, Tarby couldn't be expected to be very interested in flies and grounders at this time of year. The football season was getting underway. Lewis had seen Tarby playing football with the other boys after school. Needless to say, Tarby was always the quarterback. He threw long passes and made end runs and pulled off tricky plays, like the "Statue of Liberty."

Lewis had thought of trying to join the football game,

but he remembered what had happened back in Wisconsin. Whenever anyone charged over the line at him, he fell to the ground and covered his head with his hands. He couldn't catch passes and, if he tried to kick the ball, he usually wound up bunting it with his knee. Maybe if he got really good at baseball, he could get Tarby to teach him football next year.

But he wasn't going to learn much about baseball without Tarby. Of course, these days he wasn't learning much even with Tarby's help. On those rare occasions when Tarby showed up to play ball with Lewis, he seemed to want to get the game over with in a hurry. Lewis knew that he was losing Tarby, but so far he hadn't figured out how in the world he was going to hang on to him.

One Saturday afternoon when the two of them were poking around in the cemetery, Lewis had an idea. New Zebedee's beautiful old cemetery was on a high hill just outside of town. It was full of elaborate gravestones that showed weeping women leaning on urns and cupids extinguishing torches. There were pillars made to look as if they had been broken, and there were pillars with hands on top, pointing up. There were little tombstones made in the shape of lambs, and these were over the graves of children. Some of the lambs had been there so long that they were worn into grimy white blobs that reminded Lewis of soap.

On this particular day, Lewis and Tarby had been

inspecting a lot where all the gravestones were carved to look like wood. Each grave was marked by a little granite log, complete with bark and rings and knotholes. The curb around the lot matched the tombstones, and in the center of everything rose a broken tree of stone. The top was jagged, as if lightning had struck it, and a stone woodpecker was whetting his beak on the realistically carved bark. Lewis and Tarby had been playing in this petrified forest for a while, but now they were getting tired. The sun, red as the tomato sun in Jonathan's stained-glass window, was setting between two crooked pine trees. Lewis shivered and zipped up his jacket.

"Let's go back to my house," he said. "Mrs. Zimmermann can make us some cocoa, and I'll show you some *real* petrified wood. My uncle got it in a forest out west that was actually turned to stone."

Tarby looked bored, and he also looked mean. "Who wants to go back to your old uncle's house? It's a pretty crazy place, if you ask me. And how come old Mrs. Zimmermann is over there all the time? Is she in *luuvv* with him?" Tarby threw his arms around the stone tree and started kissing it with loud smacks. Lewis felt like crying, but somehow he managed to keep down the tears.

"I . . . I bet you think all my uncle can do is eclipse the moon," said Lewis. It sounded silly, but he couldn't think of anything else to say.

Tarby looked interested, in a bored sort of way. "Well," he said, "what else can he do?"

Lewis did not know why he said what he said next. It just came to him.

"My uncle can raise the dead."

Tarby did a somersault over one of the log-shaped markers. "Oh, sure he can," he snorted. "Look, your uncle is a fake. That night when he made it look like the moon had gone out and all that other stuff was happening, he just had us *hypnotized*. My dad told me that was prob'ly what happened."

Lewis stared at him. "You said you'd never tell anyone about what we did that night. Remember? I made you promise."

Tarby looked away. "Oh, yeah, I guess I did promise. Sorry."

Both of them sat quietly for a long while. There was nothing left of the sun but a faint red afterglow. A night wind had sprung up, and it stirred the long grass on the graves. Finally Lewis got up and spoke. His voice came from way down in his throat.

"What if I were to raise a dead person by myself?"

Tarby looked at him. He giggled. "Boy, that would be some fun. I can see you runnin' down Main Street in the middle of the night with a ghost after you." Tarby got up and waved his arms. "*Woo-oooo!*" he wailed. "I am the ghost of miss-terr-reee! *Woo-oooo!*"

Lewis's face was getting red. "Wanta see me do it?"

"Yeah," said Tarby. "I do. When are you gonna do it?"

"I'll let you know," said Lewis, although he didn't have the faintest idea of what he was going to do, or when he was going to do it, or how he was going to do it. All he knew was that he had to try, if he was going to hang on to his only friend in New Zebedee.

During that week before Halloween, Lewis spent a lot of time in his uncle's study. Normally it was okay for Lewis to browse in the library, but if Jonathan had known what books Lewis was looking at now, he would have stopped him. Lewis knew this, so he always waited till Jonathan was out visiting, or raking leaves, or tying up corn shocks in the garden. When he was sure he would not be disturbed, Lewis would slide back the paneled walnut doors, tiptoe into the study, and roll the stepladder down to the section of the library wall that contained Jonathan's magic books. Jonathan had forbidden Lewis to look through these books without his permission, so Lewis felt very bad about what he was doing. He felt bad about the whole business. But he went ahead anyway.

He looked through all the strange old volumes, with their pentacles and pentagrams, their anagrams and talismans and abracadabras and long incantations printed in Old English lettering. But he spent most of his time with a big black leather volume entitled *Necromancy*. Necromancy is the branch of magic that deals with the raising of the dead. The frontispiece of the book was an engraving that showed Dr. John Dee, personal astrologer to Queen Elizabeth I of England, as he and his assistant,

Michael Kelly, raised the spirit of a dead woman in an English churchyard at midnight. The two men were standing inside a chalk circle drawn on the ground. The border of the circle was covered with strange symbols and words. Just outside the charmed circle hovered a figure in a long nightgown. On her head she wore an odd ruffly bonnet, the kind they once buried women in. Lewis kept turning back to the illustration because it frightened him. But he read the rest of the book. He read it all, and he memorized some of the charms. He even copied one of the pentagrams and the spell that went with it onto a piece of notepaper and put it in his pocket.

Halloween was a windy dark day. Lewis sat in the window of his bedroom and watched the wind strip the trees of the few ragged brown leaves that remained. He felt sad and scared. He was sad because he had disobeyed his uncle, who was always kind to him. And he felt scared because he had promised Tarby that he would meet him in the graveyard at twelve o'clock on Halloween night, so that the two of them could raise up the spirit of a dead person. Or try to. Lewis didn't think it would work, and he was kind of hoping that it wouldn't.

They had the grave all picked out. It was a mausoleum stuck into the side of the hill the graveyard was built on. Lewis didn't know anything about who was buried in the tomb. Neither did Tarby. There wasn't even a name on the door. But whatever the name was, it probably started with *O*, because there was an *O* in the triangle over the heavy old stone arch. It was a funny kind of *O*, and it looked like this:

At dinner that night, Lewis did not say much. This was odd because he usually talked his head off about everything under the sun, especially those things he didn't know anything about. Jonathan asked him if he was all right, and Lewis said that of course he was all right, anybody could see that. Jonathan and Mrs. Zimmermann exchanged worried glances and stared at him again, but Lewis went on eating with his head down. At the end of the meal, he pushed his chair back and announced that he was not going trick-or-treating, because he was too old for it.

"Does that mean that you're not coming over to my place for cider and doughnuts?" asked Mrs. Zimmermann. "Because if it does, I'll show up at midnight at the foot of your bed in my role of Grinning Griselda, the resuscitated cadaver. It's a horrible thing to see."

Lewis looked up. There was a wild look on his face, but he managed to force his mouth into a smile.

"No, Mrs. Zimmermann," he said. "I wouldn't miss one of your cider-and-doughnut parties. Not for the world.

But right now I've got to go up to my room and finish one of John L. Stoddard's books. I've gotten to the exciting part." Whereupon he jumped up, excused himself, and ran upstairs.

Jonathan looked at Mrs. Zimmermann. "I have a feeling," he said, "that something is up."

"Hooray for your lightning-quick mind," said Mrs. Zimmermann. "Yes, something is up, and *I* have a feeling that we won't know what it is till it's over with."

"Maybe not," said Jonathan as he lit his pipe. "But I can't believe that Lewis is mixed up in anything bad. And I'm certainly not going to grill him like a mean stepfather. Still, I'd like to know what he's up to."

"So would I," said Mrs. Zimmermann thoughtfully. "Do you suppose it has anything to do with Tarby? The boy's arm is healing, and he'll probably be going back to play with the other boys soon. That leaves Lewis out."

Jonathan scratched his chin. "Yes, maybe that's it," he said. "I'll have to have a talk with him. Oh, by the way, have you noticed that the clock is louder now?" He was trying to sound nonchalant, but Mrs. Zimmermann could read the look in his eyes.

"Yes," she said, trying hard to smile. "I've heard it too. And maybe if we ignore it, it'll just die down. It has before, you know. One thing for sure: you're not going to do any good by barging around the house with a crowbar, prying open the wainscot and peering between floorboards."

"I suppose not," said Jonathan, sighing. "Though I might come across the blasted thing by sheer persistence. On the other hand, that would mean wrecking the house, and I'm not quite ready to do that. Not until I have some clearer idea that the clock is something that can do us harm. And so far, I'm just guessing. I'm even guessing when I say it's a real, physical clock, and not just some illusion left here by old Isaac Izard to drive people mad."

"It's best not to think about the thing," said Mrs. Zimmermann. "Not until you have to, at any rate. You can't prepare for all the disasters that might occur in this frightening world of ours. If the devil appears or if we find that the End of the World is at hand, we'll do something."

"Mm-hmmm. We'll hide in the cellar. Come on. Let's wash the dishes."

Lewis came down from his room at ten o'clock and went next door to have cider and doughnuts. He found Jonathan and Mrs. Zimmermann waiting for him in the dining room. There was a big round oak table at one end of the long room, and it was covered with a clean checkered tablecloth. On the table stood a gallon jug of cider and a plate of powdered doughnuts, or "fried cakes," as Mrs. Zimmermann called them. At the other end of the room, a violet fire crackled in the fireplace. Purple shadows rushed back and forth over the hearthrug and, over the mantelpiece, the purple dragon in the painting seemed to writhe and squirm. He looked very fierce indeed.

"Evening, Lewis," said Jonathan. "Pull up a chair and dig in."

After Lewis had eaten two or three doughnuts and downed four big glasses of cider, Jonathan announced that tonight's entertainment would be Historical Illusions, or Famous Scenes From the Past. He asked Lewis what past scene he would most like to see.

Lewis answered immediately. "I want to see the defeat of the Spanish Armada. Not the battle scenes, because I've read all about them in John L. Stoddard. But he doesn't tell what happened when they had to sail all the way around England and Scotland to get home. I want to see that part."

"Very well," said Jonathan. "Let's go over and sit by the fire."

They got up and walked over to the fireplace, where three big comfortable chairs waited for them. When they were all settled, Jonathan pointed his pipe at the two electric candles over the mantelpiece. Slowly the power began to drain from them. They flickered and went out. Then the bulbs in the chandelier over the table began to do the same thing. It was like watching the house lights dim in a theater. Lewis felt something tickling his nostrils and his tongue. It was the smell and taste of salt. Grainy blowing mists filled the room, and Lewis found himself standing on a grassy headland. Jonathan was on his left, and Mrs. Zimmermann was on his right. Before them a cold gray sea tumbled and tossed.

"Where are we?" asked Lewis.

"We are standing on John O'Groats," said Jonathan. "It is the northernmost point in Scotland. The year is 1588, and out there is the Armada, or what is left of it. You'll need the telescope to see them."

"Telescope?" said Lewis, and then he realized that they were standing on a little stone platform behind a curving waist-high wall. It was the kind of wall you find on scenic lookout points in state parks. And mounted on the wall was a small pay telescope with a set of instructions under glass. Lewis bent over and peered at the little card, which said:

SEE THE ARMADA
Last chance this year
Deposit five shillings, if you please.

Jonathan fumbled in his vest and dug out two large silver coins. He handed them to Lewis. They were half crowns, and each one was worth two and a half shillings in old-fashioned British money. Lewis slid the coins into the slot. There was a whirring sound. He put his eye to the telescope and looked.

At first all he saw was a milky blur but, after he had fiddled with the adjusting wheel a bit, Lewis could see several big galleons ploughing sluggishly through the waves. Their sails were ripped and torn, and their tattered rigging flew about crazily in the wind. The long rows of gunports were closed tight against the battering sea, and

Lewis could see patches on the sides of three or four ships. One lumbering hulk had a cable passed around its middle, presumably to hold it together.

As Lewis watched, the ships wallowed on. Now he could see their tall ornamented sterns. Saints and bishops and dragons supported gilded window frames or clung to scrolled corners. Lewis noticed that several statues had arms or hands or heads missing. One scowling bishop was wearing his miter at a rakish tilt.

Lewis turned the telescope. Now he was looking at a strange little man. The man was pacing the quarterdeck of the biggest, richest-looking, but most badly damaged ship of all. He wore a black cape that barely reached to his knees, and he was shivering. His whiskers were long and weepy, and he looked very worried.

"Who is the man on the biggest ship?" asked Lewis.

"That," said Jonathan, "is the Duke of Medina-Sidonia. He is the Captain General of the 'Ocean Sea,' which means that he is the commander of the Armada. The whole, shot-riddled, sinking mess. I'll bet he wishes he were at home right now."

Lewis felt sorry for the poor Duke. When he was reading John L. Stoddard in bed the night before, he had wished that he could be there in the Narrow Seas, commanding a stout English galleon. He would have emptied broadside after broadside into the Duke's flagship, until she sank. But now he wanted to help the man, if he could.

While Lewis stood thinking, Jonathan tapped him on the shoulder and pointed to something Lewis had not seen before. There, mounted on the wall, stood a cannon. A brass twenty-four pounder with a wooden, step-sided carriage and ropes running from rings in the base of the carriage to rings in the wall. The ropes were to keep the gun from rolling down the hill after it fired.

"Come on, Lewis," said Jonathan, smiling. "Let's have a shot at the Armada. Isn't this what you've always wanted to do? It's all loaded and ready to fire. Come on!"

Lewis looked as if he were going to be sick. Tears came to his eyes. "Oh, no, Uncle Jonathan! I couldn't! The poor Duke and his men. Can't we do something for them?"

Jonathan stared at Lewis and rubbed his chin. "You know," he said slowly, "for a boy who loves to play at sieges and war, you are remarkably peaceable. When confronted with the real thing, that is. Fortunately for you, however, this isn't the real thing. It's an illusion, as I may have said before. We're really still in Mrs. Zimmermann's dining room with the table at one end and the purple fire at the other. If you go feel that rock there, it will feel remarkably like an armchair. The Duke and his ships out there are less real than smoke and mist, and so is that cannon. Go on. Have a shot."

Lewis brightened up now. This would be fun. A soldier appeared out of nowhere, dressed in the red costume of an English Beefeater. He handed Lewis a smoldering wick on a long rod. Lewis applied it to the touchhole of the cannon. *Boom!* The cannon jerked back against its ropes. Bitter smoke drifted past. Jonathan, who was fighting with Mrs. Zimmermann for the use of the pay telescope, said, "I think that—oh, g'wan, Florence, find your own peephole—I think . . . yes, you have brought down his fore-topgallant spritsail."

Lewis felt pleased, though he didn't know what a fore-topgallant spritsail was. The soldier reloaded, and Lewis fired again. This time he knocked a wooden bishop off the heavily ornamented poop deck. He fired several more times, and then Jonathan gestured, and another Beefeater came running up the hill carrying a wooden bucket full of sizzling, red-hot cannon balls, or "hot potatoes," as the Elizabethan sailors used to call them.

The two soldiers loaded the cannon. First they poured in a kegful of powder. Then they stuffed in wet wadding to keep the cannon ball from setting off the powder. Then came the cannon ball itself. It hissed and steamed when it touched the wadding. Lewis applied the lin-stock again, and the gun leaped backwards. He watched the cannon ball as it whizzed toward the Duke's galleon. It looked to him like a tiny insane harvest moon. When the ball hit, the ship burst into flames. The weepy-bearded Duke sailed up toward heaven, playing a harp and sitting on a powdered doughnut. And now Lewis, Jonathan, and Mrs. Zimmermann were back in the dining room by the fire.

"Well!" said Jonathan, rubbing his hands. "And what would you like to see next?"

Lewis thought a bit. He was so excited and happy that he had almost forgotten about what he had to do later that night. "I'd like to see the Battle of Waterloo," he said.

Jonathan waved his pipe and the lights went out again. Now they were standing on a muddy hillside in Belgium. The year was 1815. It was raining, a steady smoking drizzle that half hid the high hill opposite the one they were standing on. In the valley below were little red squares. As they watched, blue arrows crashed into these squares, dented them, turned them into parallelograms, trapezoids, and rhombuses, but did not break them. Little puffs of smoke sprang out on the opposite hillside. They reminded Lewis of mushrooms. Behind him he saw geysers of dirt and chipped rock fly up.

"Napoleon's artillery," said Jonathan calmly. More mushrooms sprang up on their hillside as Wellington answered with his own cannons. Rockets exploded overhead, green and blue and sizzling white, and, of course, lovely purple. Flags rose in the valley, dipped, rose, and fell again. Lewis, Jonathan, and Mrs. Zimmermann watched the whole thing from behind a low wall that looked a great deal like the wall on John O'Groats.

After what seemed like a long time, Lewis became aware of a figure standing off to their right. A tall skinny man in a cocked hat and a black cutaway coat.

Lewis recognized him immediately. It was Wellington. He looked exactly the way he did in John Clark Ridpath's *History of the World*.

Wellington scanned the horizon with his telescope. Then he sadly clicked the telescope shut and took out his watch. The watch, which resembled the one Mrs. Zimmermann wore on a chain, dinged eight times. Wellington rolled his eyes toward the sky, put his hand on his heart, and said gravely, "Oh, that Blücher or night would come!"

"Why did he say that, Uncle Jonathan?" asked Lewis. He had looked at all the illustrations in Ridpath's book, but he had never read the account of the battle.

"Blücher is a Prussian general who is coming to aid Wellington," said Jonathan. "Napoleon has sent Grouchy off to keep Blücher busy."

Lewis giggled. "Why is he called Grouchy?"

"Because that's his name," said Mrs. Zimmermann. "Only it's pronounced Groo-*shee* because it's a French name. Fat Ears here knows that, but he's trying to be funny. Well, Jonathan, do you think Wellington will win this time?"

"Dunno, Florence. Wait and see."

Since it was Jonathan's illusion and not the real battle, and since he was feeling silly that evening, he decided to let Napoleon win for a change. Night fell with a clunk like a book falling out of a bookcase, but Blücher did not come. The blue arrows sliced into the red squares, split them up, tore them to pieces. Now the blue arrows turned into an army marching up the hill, an army of tall men wearing bearskin hats that made them even taller. They had long black moustaches and carried muskets with bayonets on the end. They were coming for Wellington, who now looked very red-faced and crabby. He tore off his hat and stomped on it. He threw his watch on the ground and stomped on it too.

"Ooh-*waah!*" he screamed. "Greenwich Mean Time! Very mean time! I want to go home *now!*"

Whereupon the scene changed, and Lewis and Uncle Jonathan and Mrs. Zimmermann were back in the dark shadowy dining room by the warm fire. The purple china clock on the mantel whanged tinnily eleven times. The whole show had taken only an hour.

Jonathan got up, stretched, yawned, and suggested that they all go to bed. Lewis thanked Mrs. Zimmermann for the wonderful party and went home with Jonathan. He went upstairs to bed, but he did not sleep.

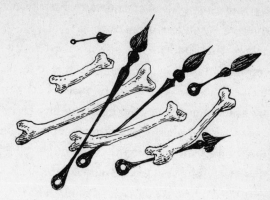

CHAPTER FIVE

As the luminous hands of his new Westclox bedside clock crept around toward midnight, Lewis lay, fully dressed, under his covers. The room was dark. His heart was pounding, and he kept saying over and over to himself, "I wish I didn't have to do it. I wish I didn't have to do it."

He felt in his pants' pocket for the piece of paper with the magic circle copied on it. There was a fat piece of yellow chalk in his other pocket. What if Uncle Jonathan came to his room to see if he were all right? He'd just have to pull the covers up to his chin and pretend that he was asleep. *Tick-tick-tick-tick.* Lewis wished that it was next week, and that he had never made his stupid promise to Tarby. He closed his eyes and stared at the patterns that formed on the insides of his eyelids.

Minutes passed. Suddenly Lewis sat up. He threw back the covers and stared at the clock. It was five minutes after twelve! He had promised to meet Tarby in the cemetery at midnight, and now he was going to be late! What could he do? Tarby wouldn't wait for him. He would go home, and tomorrow he would tell all his friends how Lewis had chickened out.

Lewis rubbed his face and tried to think. The cemetery stood atop a long ridge that rose just on the other side of Wilder Creek Park. You had to walk half a mile beyond the city limits to get to the road that ran up the ridge. There was a short cut, of course, but Lewis hadn't intended to take it. Now he had no choice.

Slowly, carefully, Lewis eased himself down onto the floor. He knelt down and groped under the bed for his flashlight. It was a long, old-fashioned flashlight with a fluted handle and a big round lamp on the end. The metal felt cold and slimy in his hand. He went to the closet and put on his heavy jacket. It would be cold up on Cemetery Hill.

Lewis opened the bedroom door. The hall was dark, as usual, and from the next room he could hear Uncle Jonathan snoring. Lewis felt awful. It was like being sick to your stomach. He wished with all his heart that he could run into Jonathan's room, wake him up, and tell him all about the adventure he was going on, and why he had to go through with it. But he didn't do any of these things. Instead, he tiptoed across the hall and opened the door that led to the back stairs.

It didn't take long for Lewis to get to the other side of town. When he had reached the CITY LIMITS sign, he poked around by the side of the road until he found a little wooden staircase that ran down the gravel bank to Wilder Creek Park. The creek was fairly shallow at this point, so Lewis waded across. The water was freezing on his ankles. When he got to the other side he looked up. His hands felt sweaty, and he almost turned around and went home.

He was looking at Cemetery Hill. It was a high, flat-topped ridge cut across in two places by a narrow dirt road. It wasn't a hard hill to climb: New Zebedee children went up and down it every day during the summer. But to Lewis, who was scared of heights, it might as well have been Mount Everest.

Lewis looked up at the dark hill, and he swallowed a couple of times. Maybe if he took the long way around . . . no, he was already late, and Tarby might get bored and go home. The last thing Lewis wanted was to be in the cemetery alone at this time of night. He got a tight grip on his flashlight and started to climb.

At the first landing, Lewis stopped. He was breathing hard, and the front of his jacket was soaked through.

There were black smudges on the knees of his trousers, and there was a twig in his shoe. Two more stages. Lewis gritted his teeth and went on.

At the top of the hill, he dropped to his knees and crossed himself several times. The sweat was running down his face, and he could feel his heart thumping. Well, he had done it. It was no great triumph because Tarby had probably scaled the ridge in a tenth of the time it had taken him. But at least he had done it.

Lewis looked around. He was standing at the edge of a long avenue lined with willow trees. The bare strings of the willows swayed in the wind, and Lewis shivered. He felt very cold and very alone. At the far end of the avenue, the gray gate of the cemetery glimmered. Lewis started to walk toward it.

The cemetery gate was a heavy arch of stone covered with elaborate carving. On the lintel were inscribed these words:

THE TRUMPET SHALL SOUND

AND

THE DEAD SHALL BE RAISED

Lewis pushed open the squeaky iron gate and walked quickly past the rows of white headstones. The mausoleum was on the other side of Cemetery Hill, the side that looked out across the deep valley beyond the town. A little narrow path led down to the stone platform in front of the tomb door. Where was Tarby?

As Lewis looked around, someone said, "Boo!" Lewis almost fainted. It was Tarby, of course, hiding in the shadow of the stone arch on the front of the mausoleum.

"Hi! You sure took long enough," said Tarby. "Where were you?"

"It was hard work climbing," said Lewis, staring sadly down at his wet and dirty trousers.

"It's always hard climbing for fatsoes," said Tarby. "Whyncha lose some weight?"

"Come on, let's do what we're supposed to be doing," said Lewis. He felt depressed.

The cracked and mossy stone slab that lay at the doorstep of the tomb was in the shadow of the hillside now. Everything around it lay in bright moonlight. Lewis turned on the flashlight and played the pale beam over the ugly iron doors. A heavy chain held the doors together, and it was fastened by a large, heart-shaped padlock. Lewis flashed the beam up. There was the strange-looking *O* on the cornice. The wind had died down. Everything was quiet. Lewis handed the flashlight to Tarby and knelt down. Out came the scrap of paper and the chalk. He drew a big circle and then a smaller one within it, like this:

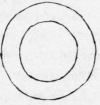

As Tarby held the flashlight steady, Lewis filled in the border of the magic circle with symbols from the piece of paper. When he had chalked in the last strange sign, there was still a blank space in the border. Lewis had read in Jonathan's book that you were supposed to fill in the space with the name of the dead person. But he didn't know the name.

"Well," said Tarby, "I don't see any dead people."

"It's not finished," said Lewis. "We've got to put in the name."

Tarby looked disgusted. "You mean you don't know it?"

"No, I don't," sighed Lewis. "Maybe if we sit here for a minute or two it will come to us."

They knelt silently at the door of the tomb. A sudden gust of wind rattled the dead leaves on an oak tree that grew nearby. Minutes passed. Lewis's mind was completely blank. Then, for some reason, he picked up the chalk.

"Hold the flashlight down here," he said.

Slowly, carefully, he spelled out a name. The funny thing was that he was not thinking of a name at all. It was as if someone else was guiding his hand. With one last down-stroke of the chalk he completed the word: *Selenna*. It was a strange name. Lewis had never known anyone called Selenna. He didn't even know how to pronounce the name. But there it was.

He stood up with the creased paper in his hand. Now

he started to chant in a high-pitched nervous voice: *Aba bēbē bachabē* . . .

He stopped. Tarby, who was crouched beside him, grabbed his arm and squeezed it hard. From deep within the tomb came a sound. *Boom!* A deep hollow sound. The iron doors jolted, as if they had been struck a blow from inside. The chain rattled, and there was a *clunk* on the pavement. The padlock had fallen off. And now, as the boys knelt, terrified, two small spots of freezing gray light appeared. They hovered and danced before the doors of the tomb, which now stood ajar. And something black—blacker than the night, blacker than ink spilled into water—was oozing from the space between the doors.

Tarby shook Lewis and squeezed his arm harder. "Run!" he shouted.

They tumbled over the bank and started to scramble down the hillside. Part of the way Lewis slid on his belly, with roots scratching at his face. He clawed at the wet slippery grass, but he could not get a handhold. Then he was tumbling over and over, and then he was sliding on his back. Rocks scraped his shoulder blades and bumped the back of his head. And then he was sitting on the dirt road, thoroughly shaken and sick and scared.

The moon drifted out from behind a thin veil of clouds and stared down at Lewis as if it were scared too. Tarby was sprawled near him in a weedy ditch. He got up quickly and stared back up the hillside. Now he was tugging at Lewis's arm. "Come on! We've got to get out

of here! It might come after us! Oh, come on! Please come on!"

Lewis was dazed and shaken, but he got up and followed Tarby over the next stage of the hillside, and the next one. They waded across the stream and were soon on the gravel road that led back to New Zebedee.

As they walked along, Lewis kept stopping and shuddering. Tarby told him to quit it.

"I can't help it," said Lewis in a sick voice. "Did you see it? It was awful!"

"I don't know what I saw," said Tarby sullenly. "Maybe it was the moonlight or something."

Lewis stared at him. Was Tarby kidding, or was he trying to deny to himself that he had seen what he really had seen? Lewis didn't know, and he didn't care. All he knew was that he was terribly frightened.

Lewis sneaked back into the house a little before three A.M. He tiptoed up the back stairs, checked to make sure that his uncle was asleep—he was—and quietly opened the door of his own room. Just as quietly, he shut it behind him. Then he slowly began to strip off his wet and dirty clothes, which he wadded up and threw into a dark corner of his closet. Where was his flashlight? Tarby must have taken it. He would get it back from him later. As for the clothes, he could get them cleaned without Jonathan knowing about it.

Lewis went to bed. He tried to sleep, but all he could see when he closed his eyes were those two burning circles of light. Finally he did drift off, but he had a strange dream. Clock hands and skeleton bones were chasing him around and around a high stone tomb. Lewis awoke with a start and, for a moment, it seemed that his room, and the whole house, was filled with a loud ticking noise.

CHAPTER SIX

The next morning, when Lewis came down to breakfast, Uncle Jonathan was reading an article on the front page of the New Zebedee *Chronicle*. Curious, Lewis leaned over his shoulder and this is what he read:

TOMB DESECRATED BY VANDALS

Answers Sought to Senseless Act

Last night vandals broke into the Old Izard mausoleum in Oakridge Cemetery. The doors of the tomb were found standing ajar, with the padlock lying shattered on the pavement. This incident has sadly marred what was otherwise a Halloween remarkably free from incidents of vandalism and wanton destructiveness. What these human ghouls hoped to attain lies mercifully beyond conjecture, but it may be hoped . . .

"Morning, Lewis," said Jonathan, without looking up. "Did you sleep well?"

Lewis turned pale. Did Jonathan know?

Mrs. Zimmermann was sitting across the table, munching her Cheerios. "Does it say whether they disturbed the coffins?" she asked.

"No, it doesn't," said Jonathan. "The caretaker probably just shoved the doors shut and fastened them with a new padlock. I don't blame him. I wouldn't want to look inside old Isaac Izard's tomb."

Lewis sat down. There were too many things whirling around in his head, and he was trying to get them straightened out.

"I . . . I was up in the cemetery with Tarby a couple of times, Uncle Jonathan," he said cautiously, "but I didn't see any tomb with 'Izard' on it."

"Oh, well, he didn't want his name on the tomb. When he had it fixed up for his wife's body, he brought in a stonecutter who chiseled off the family name and carved an omega."

"An omega?" said Lewis. "What's that?"

"It's the last letter of the Greek alphabet, and it's used a lot by wizards. It looks like an *O*, except that it's open at the bottom. It is the sign of the Last Judgment—the End of the World."

Lewis sat there staring at the little *O*'s floating in his bowl. He forced himself to eat a few of them.

"How come he wanted something like that on his tomb?" asked Lewis. He was trying to conceal the tremble in his voice.

"Lord knows, Lewis," said Jonathan. "Say, you're not scared about this tomb-breaking business, are you? Old Isaac Izard's dead and gone. He's not going to bother us."

Lewis looked at Jonathan. Then he looked at Mrs. Zimmermann. He knew, as well as he knew anything, that they couldn't wait for him to go off to school so they could discuss the matter alone. So he finished his breakfast, mumbled goodby to them both, grabbed up his books, and left.

Jonathan and Mrs. Zimmermann did indeed want to discuss the break-in alone. Any tampering with the tomb of two powerful wizards like Isaac and Selenna Izard was a matter for serious discussion, and they didn't want to frighten Lewis with their talk. But they had no idea of what Lewis had done. Jonathan was not in the habit of peering in at the sleeping form of his nephew during the night, so he had no idea that Lewis had been out of the house. Of course, he and Mrs. Zimmermann had been concerned for some time about Lewis's strange behavior. But they did not connect it with what had happened on Halloween night.

After their discussion—which came to no conclusions at all, except that there was dirty work afoot—Jonathan and Mrs. Zimmermann decided that it would be nice to take Lewis on an evening ride around Capharnaum County. They knew he loved to ride, and since they hadn't taken him out in some time, they thought that maybe an excursion would shake some of the gloom out of his system.

But when Lewis came home from school that day, he was depressed and worried. He had been thinking about the tomb business all day long. So, when Jonathan pushed back his chair after dinner and asked Lewis if he'd like to go for a nice long ride, Lewis merely shrugged his shoulders and said, "Yeah, I guess I'd like to go" in a dying-cat sort of voice.

Jonathan stared at Lewis for a minute, but he said nothing. He merely got up and went to get his car keys. Soon all three of them—Jonathan, Mrs. Zimmermann, and Lewis—were crammed into the front seat of Jonathan's 1935 Muggins Simoon, a big black car with running boards and a windshield that could be cranked open. The car, spewing clouds of bluish smoke, backed down the rutted driveway and into the street.

They drove for hours, as the afterglow of sunset stayed and stayed, and the hollows filled with purple mist. They drove past barns with big blue signs on their sides that said: CHEW MAIL POUCH. They drove past green John Deere tractors parked in deep muddy ruts. Up hill and down hill they drove, over bumpy railroad crossings with X-shaped signs that said: RAIL-SING CROS-ROAD if you read them the wrong way, through little towns that were no more than a church, a food store with a gas pump outside, and a flagpole on a triangle of green grass where the roads met. By the time it got dark, they were miles from New Zebedee.

They were on their way home when—for no reason that Lewis could see—Jonathan stopped the car. He turned off the motor and sat there staring at the row of green dashboard lights.

"What's wrong, Uncle Jonathan?" asked Lewis.

"I keep imagining that I hear a car somewhere," said Jonathan. "Do you hear it, Florence?"

"Yes, I do," said Mrs. Zimmermann, giving him a puzzled look. "But what's so odd about that? They do let people drive these roads at night, you know."

"Do they?" said Jonathan in a strange voice. He opened the car door and stepped out onto the gravel. "Stay here," he said to them. He walked up the road a little ways and stood there, listening. Even with the car door open, Lewis could hear nothing but the wind in the roadside trees and the clattering of a tin sign on a barbed-wire fence. The car was parked near the top of a high hill, and now Lewis could see headlights rising out of a gully and then dipping into the next one.

Jonathan came running back to the car. He slammed the door and started the motor. With a squealing of tires, he turned the car around and headed back the way they had come.

Lewis was frightened. "What's wrong, Uncle Jonathan?" he asked.

"Ask me later, Lewis. Florence, what's the best way—other way—back to New Zebedee?"

"Take the next side road to your right. That's Twelve Mile Road, and it runs into the Wilder Creek Road. And step on it. They're gaining."

Many times, when he had been out riding with his father and mother, Lewis had pretended that they were being followed by some car or other. It was a good game to pass the time on long dull evening rides, and he remembered how he had always felt disappointed when the mystery car turned away into a side street or a driveway. But tonight the game was for real.

Around sharp curves they went, lurching dangerously far over and squealing the tires. Up hills, down hills, then seventy or eighty miles an hour on the straightaway, which was never straight for long on these winding country roads. Lewis had never seen Jonathan drive so fast, or so recklessly. But no matter how fast he drove, the two cold circles of light still burned in his rear-view mirror.

Both Mrs. Zimmermann and Uncle Jonathan seemed to know who or what was in the car behind them—or at least they seemed to know that it was someone that had the power to do them harm. But they said as little as possible, except to confer now and then about directions. So Lewis just sat there, trying to feel comforted by the green dashboard lights and the warm breath of the heater on his knees. Of course, he also felt comforted by the two wizards, whose warm friendly bodies pressed against his in the furry darkness. But he knew that they were scared, and this made him twice as scared.

What was after them? Why didn't Uncle Jonathan or Mrs. Zimmermann just wave an arm and turn the evil car into a wad of smoldering tinfoil? Lewis stared up at the reflected headlights, and he thought of what he had seen in the cemetery, and of what Uncle Jonathan had told him about Mrs. Izard's eyeglasses. He was beginning to have a theory about how all these things fitted together.

The car raced on, spitting stones from under its tires. Down into hollows bordered by dark skeletal trees, up over high hills, on and on while the setting moon seemed to race to keep up with them. They covered a large part of Capharnaum County that night, because the way around was a long way. After what seemed like hours of driving, they came to a place where three roads met. As the car screeched around the turn, Lewis saw—for a few seconds—a Civil War cannon white with frost, a wooden church with smeary stained-glass windows, and a general store with a dark glimmering window that said: SALADA.

"We're on the Wilder Creek Road now, Lewis," said

Mrs. Zimmermann as she put her arm around him. "It won't be long now. Don't be afraid."

The car raced on. Dead roadside stalks bent in its hot wind, and overhanging branches whipped along the metal roof. The burning white holes danced in the mirror as before, and it looked like they were getting closer. They had never, since the start of the chase, been more than two or three car lengths away.

Jonathan shoved the accelerator to the floor. The needle moved up to eighty, which was dangerous, to say the least, on these roads. But the greater danger was behind, so Jonathan took the big roundhouse curves as well as he could, and the tires screeched, and the fenders almost touched the crumbling asphalt at the side of the road. This was blacktop, and you could go faster on it than you could on loose gravel.

At last they came to the top of a high hill and, there below them, glimmering peacefully in the starlight—the moon had gone down some time ago—was Wilder Creek. There was the bridge, a maze of crisscrossing black girders. Down the hill they barreled, faster and faster. The car behind followed, just as fast. They were almost to the bridge when the lights in the rear-view mirror did something headlights had never done before. They grew and brightened till the reflection was a blinding bar of white light. Lewis clapped his hands to his eyes. Had he been struck blind? Had Jonathan been blinded too? Would the car crash, or . . .

Suddenly Lewis heard the rolling clatter of the bridge boards under the car. He took his hands away from his face. He could see. Jonathan was smiling and putting on the brakes. Mrs. Zimmermann heaved a deep sigh of relief. They were across the bridge.

As Jonathan opened the door to get out, Lewis twisted around in his seat and saw that the other car had stopped just before it got to the bridge. Its headlights were dark now, except for two smoldering yellow pinpoints. Lewis could not tell if there was anyone in the car, because the windshield was covered by a blank silvery sheen.

Jonathan stood there, his hands on his hips, watching. He did not seem to be afraid of the other car now. Slowly the mysterious car turned around and drove away. When Jonathan got back to the Muggins Simoon he was chuckling.

"It's all over, Lewis. Relax. Witches and other evil things can't cross running water. It's an old rule, but it still applies."

"You might throw in the fact," said Mrs. Zimmermann in her most pedantic tone, "that Elihu Clabbernong built that iron bridge in 1892. He was supposed to be doing it for the county, but he was really trying to make sure that the ghost of his dead uncle, Jedediah, didn't cross the stream to get him. Now Elihu was a part-time warlock, and what he put into the iron of the bridge . . ."

"Oh, good heavens!" cried Jonathan, covering his ears.

"Are you going to go through the whole history of Capharnaum County at four A.M.?"

"Is it *that* late?" asked Lewis.

"That late or later," said Jonathan wearily. "It's been quite a ride."

They drove on toward New Zebedee. On the way they stopped at an all-night diner and had a large breakfast of waffles, eggs, American fries, sausage, coffee, and milk. Then they sat around for a long time talking about the narrow escape they had just had. Lewis asked a lot of questions, but he didn't get many answers.

When they got back to New Zebedee, it was dawn. Dawn of an overcast November day. The town and its hills appeared to be swimming in a gray grainy murk. When Jonathan pulled up in front of his house he said, "There's something wrong, Florence. Stay in the car with Lewis."

"Oh, dear!" she cried, wrinkling up her mouth. "What more can happen?"

Jonathan swung back the iron gate and marched up the walk. From where he was sitting, Lewis could see that the front door was open. This could easily be explained, since people in New Zebedee never locked their doors, and sometimes the latches didn't hold when they closed them. Jonathan disappeared into the house, and he didn't come back for ten full minutes. When he did reappear, he looked worried.

"Come on, Florence," he said, opening the door on her side. "It's safe to go in, I think. But the house has been broken into."

Lewis burst into tears. "They didn't steal your water-pipe, did they? Or the Bon-Sour coins?"

Jonathan smiled weakly. "No, Lewis, I'm afraid it's not as simple as all that. Someone was looking for something, and I think they found it. Come on in."

Lewis expected to find the house in wild disorder, with chairs and lamps smashed and things all scattered around. But when he got to the front hall, he found everything in order. At least, that's the way it looked. Jonathan tapped him on the shoulder and pointed toward the ceiling. "Look up there," he said.

Lewis gasped. The brass cup that covered the place where the ceiling fixture met the ceiling had been pried loose. It dangled halfway down the chain.

"It's like that all over the house," said Jonathan. "Every wall sconce and ceiling light has had its cup jimmied loose. A few chairs were overturned and a couple of vases were broken, just to make it look like this was an ordinary break-in. But we ought not to be fooled. Whoever it was had a general idea of where to look. Come here."

Jonathan led Lewis and Mrs. Zimmermann into the front parlor, a more or less unused room full of fussy little red-velvet chairs and settees. On the wall over the parlor organ was a brass light fixture like all the others in the house: a tarnished cup-shaped thing fitted to the wall, and a crooked little brass tube sticking out of it. On the end of the tube was a socket and a bulb with a frilly pink shade.

"I thought you said the cup was loose," said Lewis.

"It was. It is," said Jonathan. "In this case Whosis tried to fit it back just the way it was, which was kind of stupid, seeing as how all the other cups in the house are at half mast. Some of them are slid all the way down to the socket. But I think Whosis was trying, in a clumsy way, to keep me from looking too closely at this one."

Jonathan pulled over a chair and stood up on it. He slid the cup out and peered inside. Then he got down and went to the cellarway for a flashlight. When he got back, Mrs. Zimmermann and Lewis had taken turns looking into the cup. They both were puzzled. What they saw inside the dusty bowl was a greenish rust blot. It reminded Lewis of the stuff in the cracks and crevices of the copper Roman coins they played poker with. It was the mark of something that had lain concealed inside the old brass cup for a long, long time. The mark looked like this:

"It looks like a clock key," said Lewis in a weak, throaty voice.

"Yes, it does," said Jonathan. He played the light around inside the cup and squinted hard.

"Uncle Jonathan, what does all this mean?" Lewis sounded as if he were about to burst into tears.

"I wish I knew," said Jonathan. "I really wish I knew."

CHAPTER SEVEN

It rained a lot in New Zebedee that November. Cold rain fell steadily through each night and left the sidewalk a glaze of ice in the morning. Lewis sat in his window seat and watched the rain peck at the chipped slates of the front porch roof. He felt sick inside. It was an empty, black feeling in the pit of his stomach. He was eaten up with guilt and remorse because he knew what he had done—or thought he knew, at any rate. He had let Mrs. Izard out of her tomb, and now she had stolen the key. The key that wound up the magic clock ticking in the walls of Jonathan's house, ticking away morning, noon, and night; sometimes loud, sometimes soft, but always there.

What was going to happen? How could anyone stop her? Had she used the key? What would happen if she did? Lewis had no answers for any of these questions.

It might have helped if he had been able to talk the whole matter over with Jonathan, but then he would have had to admit what he had done. And Lewis was afraid to do that. It was not that Uncle Jonathan was such a hard man to talk to. He was easier to talk to than most people Lewis knew, easier by far than Lewis's own father had ever been. Then, why was Lewis afraid?

Well, he was afraid because he was afraid. Maybe it was because his mother had once threatened to send him to the Detention Home when he was bad. The Detention Home was a big white house on the outskirts of the town that Lewis and his parents had lived in. It stood on a high hill and had bars and chicken wire over the windows. Bad boys and girls were sent there—at least, that's what everyone said. Lewis had never known anyone who had actually gotten sent there. Of course, Lewis's mother would never have sent him there for being bad. Not really. But Lewis didn't know that, and now when Lewis thought of telling his uncle about Halloween night, he thought of the Detention Home, and he was afraid. It wasn't a reasonable fear, considering the kind of man Jonathan was. But Lewis had not known him for very long, and anyway, people are not always so reasonable.

And there was another thing that added to Lewis's despair. He had lost Tarby. He had lost him in spite of all his sneaking and planning—or maybe he had lost him because of it. It was one thing to say that you could raise the dead, but when you did it—well, ordinary people have never cared much for the company of wizards. Tarby was afraid of Lewis now, or else he was enjoying himself with the other boys, the boys who could hit home runs and catch fly balls. Whichever way it was, Lewis had not seen Tarby since Halloween night.

The month wore on, the rain kept falling, and nothing mysterious or evil happened. Until one day—the third of December it was—when the Hanchetts moved out.

The Hanchetts lived across the street from Uncle Jonathan in a boxy, dark-brown house with tiny windows, the kind of windows that have little diamond-shaped panes and swing out instead of sliding up and down. The Hanchetts were a friendly, middle-aged couple, and they liked Jonathan and Mrs. Zimmermann a lot, but one morning they were gone. A couple of days after their disappearance a truck came and a couple of movers in gray uniforms packed all the Hanchetts' furniture into it, and drove off. A real-estate man came around and hung a big red and white sign on their front door. The sign said:

HI THERE!

I'M FOR SALE

Call Bishop Barlow Realtors

Phone: 865

Bishop Barlow was not a real bishop. Bishop was just his first name. Lewis knew the man: he was a fat loud-mouth who wore sunglasses all the time, even on rainy days. He smoked cheap smelly cigars and wore sports coats that looked like awnings.

Jonathan seemed really upset at the departure of the Hanchetts. He phoned their son, who was a lawyer in Osee Five Hills, and he found out that the Hanchetts were living with him. The frightened couple would not talk to Jonathan over the phone, and they seemed to blame him for whatever had made them leave. The son did not seem to know much about the matter. He muttered something about ghosts and "messing around with magic" and hung up.

One day Lewis was walking home from school when he saw a small moving van pull up in front of the empty Hanchett house. The big black letters on the side of the van said: TERMINUS MOVERS INC. Lewis was about to cross the street to watch the men unload the truck when he realized, with a shock, that he knew the driver. It was Hammerhandle.

All the children in New Zebedee knew Hammerhandle and, if they were smart, they were afraid of him. He was a mean old hobo who lived in a tar-paper shack down by the railroad tracks, and he had a reputation for being able to foretell the future. Lewis had stood once on the outskirts of a crowd of kids gathered about the door of Hammerhandle's shack on a hot summer day. He remembered seeing Hammerhandle seated in the doorway on a broken kitchen chair. He was telling stories about the World's Last Night, which, if you believed him, was not far off. Behind Hammerhandle, in the disorder and darkness of the old shack, stood ranks of smooth yellow poles: ax handles, hoe handles, hammer handles. He made them and sold them. That was how he got his name.

Lewis stood there wondering what he was doing driving a moving van. Hammerhandle slammed the door on the driver's side and walked across the street. He looked around him quickly and then grabbed Lewis by the collar. His bristly face was close to Lewis's now, and his breath smelled of whiskey and tobacco.

"What the hell you starin' at, kid?"

"N-nothing. I-I just like to watch people moving in." It was getting dark, and Lewis wondered if anyone could see him. If he yelled, would Jonathan or Mrs. Zimmermann come?

Hammerhandle let go of Lewis's collar. "Look, kid," he said in his harsh scraping voice, "you just keep yer nose on your side of the fence, okay? An' that goes f'ya fat uncle too. Just don't bother me, okay?" He glared at Lewis, turned, and went back to the truck.

Lewis stood there trembling for a few moments. He was sweating all over. Then he turned and ran in through the open gate, up the walk, and into the house.

"Uncle Jonathan! Uncle Jonathan!" he shouted. He

yanked open the doors of the study and looked. No Jonathan. He shouted into the front parlor and into the kitchen and up the stairwell. At last Uncle Jonathan appeared at the top of the stairs. He was wearing his bathrobe, which was made in the shape of the robes professors wear at graduation ceremonies, black with red stripes on the sleeves. In one hand he held a dripping, long-handled scrub brush. In the other, he held the book he had been reading in the tub.

"Yes, Lewis? What is it?" He sounded cross at first, but when he saw the state that Lewis was in, he dropped the book and the brush and clumped down the stairs to throw his arms around the boy. It was a damp embrace, but it felt good to Lewis.

"Lewis, my boy!" said Jonathan, kneeling in front of him. "What in the name of heaven is wrong? You look awful!"

Lewis, stuttering and breaking down several times, told Jonathan what had happened. When he was through, he watched Jonathan's expression change. There was a hard, angry look on his face now, but his anger was not directed at Lewis. He stood up, knotted his bathrobe tighter about him, and stalked to the front door. For a minute Lewis thought that Jonathan was going out to challenge Hammerhandle right then and there. But he merely opened the front door and stared across at the Hanchett house. The workmen were just hitching up the tail gate and getting ready to drive off. Apparently there hadn't been much to unload.

With folded arms Jonathan watched the truck drive away. "I might have known he'd be in on it," he said bitterly. Lewis stared up at his uncle. He didn't have the faintest idea of what was going on, and for some reason he was afraid to ask what Jonathan meant.

That evening at supper, Lewis asked Jonathan why Hammerhandle had acted so mean. Jonathan threw down his fork and said angrily, "Because he's mean, that's why! Do you have to have explanations? Just stay away from him and you'll be all right. And stay away . . . stay away . . . oh, I don't know what I mean!" He got up and stomped out of the room. Lewis heard the study doors slam.

Mrs. Zimmermann reached across the table and laid her hand gently on Lewis's. "Don't worry, Lewis," she said. "He's not angry at you. But he does have a lot on his mind these days, and he hasn't been getting much sleep. Come on over to my house and we'll have a game of chess."

"Okay." Lewis was grateful for the suggestion.

They played chess till ten o'clock at night and, since Lewis won most of the games, he was in a happy mood when he went home. Upstairs he saw a line of light under the door of Jonathan's bedroom. He decided not to disturb him. When he had gotten ready for bed, Lewis

went to his window seat, sat down, and pulled back the heavy curtain.

It was a bright, cold, starry night. The water tower at the top of the hill glimmered in the moonlight, and the roofs of the houses were dark pointed shadows. There were lights on in the houses that stood on either side of the Hanchett house and, in one window, Lewis saw the gray aquarium-glow of one of those new television sets. Jonathan hadn't gotten one yet. The Hanchett house seemed to lie in deep shadow, except for faint patches of moonlight on the roof. By the light of a street lamp, Lewis could see that there was a car parked in the driveway.

He was about to close the curtain and go to bed when the porch light of the Hanchett house came on. The two frosted panes of the front door glowed yellow. Then one of the panels of the door moved inward. Someone stepped out onto the front stoop. Lewis watched as who-ever-it-was stood there, just stood there, taking in the frosty air of the December night. He thought he caught the faint glitter of spectacles, but he couldn't be sure at this distance.

After a little while, the dark figure went inside and pushed the door shut. The hall light went out. Lewis sat there for a while thinking, then he lowered the curtain and went to bed.

CHAPTER EIGHT

The next day Jonathan was helping Lewis rummage in the front hall closet for his ice skates. Lewis had weak ankles, and he was terrified of falling down on the ice, but he had decided to try to learn to skate. If he got good enough he might be able to worm his way back into Tarby's favor. He had never seen Tarby ice skate, but he was sure that the team's greatest home-run hitter was also the champion ice skater of New Zebedee. He probably could sign his name across the ice of Durgy's Pond.

So Lewis and Jonathan threw warped badminton rackets, raccoon coats, galoshes, and picnic baskets into the hall. Finally Jonathan came up with what looked like a short aluminum ski for a midget. It was a beginner's skate, with two little ridges for runners.

"This it?"

"That's one of them. Thanks a lot, Uncle Jonathan. Now all we need is the other."

As they went on searching Lewis said, in what he thought was a casual way, "Who's living in the old Hanchett house?"

Jonathan stood up suddenly in the closet and banged his head on a shelf. When he had stopped rubbing his head and wincing, he looked down at Lewis and said, rather sharply, "Why do you want to know?"

"I just wanted to know," said Lewis shyly. Once again, he wondered what his uncle was angry about.

Jonathan stepped out of the closet with the other skate. He dropped it into a pile of clothes.

"So you just wanted to know, eh? Well, Lewis, there are some things it would be better for you *not* to know. So if you'll take my advice, you'll just stop poking around where you're not wanted. There's your other skate and . . . and good day. I have work to do in the study, and I've already wasted enough time answering your foolish questions."

Jonathan got up abruptly and stalked off to the study. He had slid back the doors with a loud clatter when he paused and went back to the closet, where Lewis was still kneeling with tears in his eyes.

"Please forgive me, Lewis," said Jonathan in a tired

voice. "I've been feeling really rotten lately. Too many cigars, I guess. As for the house across the street, I hear that it's been rented to an old lady named Mrs. O'Meagher. She acts kind of crabby—or so I'm told. I really haven't met her, and . . . and I just didn't want anything bad to happen to you." Jonathan smiled nervously and patted Lewis on the shoulder. Then he got up and walked to the door of the study. Again he stopped.

"Don't go over there," he said quickly, and then he stepped inside and slammed the double doors, hard.

Lewis felt crisscrossing lines of mystery and fear and tension hemming him in on all sides. He had never seen his uncle acting like this. And he wondered, more than ever, about the new neighbor across the street.

One night during the week before Christmas, after a heavy snow had fallen, Lewis was awakened by the sound of the doorbell ringing. *Brr-rr-rring! Brr-rr-rring!* It was not an electric bell, but an old, tired mechanical bell set in the middle of the front door. Someone was turning the flat metal key, grinding the stiff old chimes around. *Brr-rr-rring!*

Lewis sat up and looked at his bedside clock. The two luminous hands were straight up. Midnight! Who could it be at this hour? Maybe Uncle Jonathan would go down and answer it. Lewis felt cold just thinking of the drafty front hall. He bundled his quilt about him and shivered.

The bell rang again. It sounded like a whiny person

insisting on some stupid point in an argument. No sound from Jonathan's room. No waking-up sounds, that is. Lewis could hear his uncle's loud, steady snoring even though there was a thick wall between their rooms. Jonathan could sleep through an artillery bombardment.

Lewis got up. He threw back the covers, slipped on his bathrobe, and found his slippers. Quietly, he padded down the hall and then down the dark staircase. At the entrance to the front hall he stopped. There was a street-light burning just outside the front gate, and it threw a bent black shadow against the pleated curtain on the front door. Lewis stood still and watched the shadow. It didn't move. Slowly he began to walk forward. When he reached the door, he closed his fingers around the cold knob and turned it. The door rattled open, and a freezing wind blew in over his bare ankles. There stood his Aunt Mattie, who was dead.

Lewis stepped back as the old woman, her head cocked to one side as it always had been, tottered across the floor toward him. A shaking blue light filled the air around her, and Lewis, his eyes wide open in this nightmare, saw Aunt Mattie as she had been the last time he had seen her alive. Her dress was black and wrinkled, she wore heavy shoes with thick heels, and she tapped her bunchy, black umbrella as she went. Lewis even thought he smelled kerosene—her house, her furniture, and her clothing had always reeked of it. The white fungus blotch that was her face shook and glowed as she said, in a horribly familiar voice, "Well, Lewis? Aren't you glad to see me?"

Lewis fainted. When he awoke, he was lying on his back in the cold hallway. The shaking blue light was gone. So was Aunt Mattie, though the front door was open. Skitters of snow blew in over the worn threshold, and the street lamp burned quiet and cold across the street. Had it all been a sleepwalker's dream?

Lewis didn't think so. He had never been a sleepwalker before. He stood there thinking for a minute, and then, for some reason, he shuffled out onto the front porch and started to pick his way down the snow-covered steps. His feet were so cold that they stung, but he kept going until he was halfway down the walk. Then he turned and looked at the house. He gasped. There were strange lights playing over the blank windows and the rough sandstone walls. They wouldn't have been strange lights at midday in the summer, but on a December night they were eerie. For they were leaf-lights, the shifting circles and crescents cast by sunlight falling through leaves.

Lewis stood and stared for several minutes. Then the lights faded, and he was alone in the dark, snow-covered yard. The chestnut tree dropped a light dusting of snow on his head, shaking him out of his trance. His feet were numb and tingling, and he felt, for the first time, the cold wind whipping through his thin pajamas and his half-open cotton bathrobe. Shuddering, Lewis stumbled back up the walk.

When he got to his room, he sat down on the edge of his bed. He knew he wasn't going back to sleep. There were the makings of a fire in his fireplace, and he knew where the cocoa was kept. A few minutes later Lewis was sitting by a warm, cheerful fire that cast cozy shadows over the black marble of his own personal fireplace. He sipped steaming cocoa from a heavy earthenware mug and tried to think pleasant thoughts. None came to him. After an hour of sitting and sipping and brooding, he plugged in the floor lamp, got John L. Stoddard's second lecture on China out of the bookcase, and sat reading by the fire until dawn.

The next morning at breakfast, Lewis saw that Jonathan was red-eyed and nervous acting. Had his sleep been disturbed too? Jonathan had not discussed the break-in or the car chase or the Izard tomb with Lewis, and Lewis was not about to bring up any of these subjects. But he knew that something was bothering Jonathan, and he also knew that, ever since the night of the break-in, Jonathan and Mrs. Zimmermann had been holding midnight conferences. He had heard their voices coming up through the hot-air register, although he had never been able to make out what was being said. He had thought a couple of times of hiding in the secret passageway, but he was afraid of getting caught. A passage that is entered through a china cupboard full of rattling dishes is not as secret as one might wish. And if some secret spring lock snapped shut on him, he would need to scream his way out, and then there would have to be explanations.

Lewis almost wished that something like that would happen, because he was sick of his secret. He was sick of it because it kept him away from Jonathan and Mrs. Zimmermann. He always felt that they were watching him, waiting for him to break down and tell them everything. How much did they know?

Christmas at 100 High Street was both good and bad that year. There was a big tree in the study and the glass balls on it were magic. Sometimes they reflected the room, and sometimes they showed you ancient ruins on unknown planets. Jonathan gave Lewis several magic toys, including a large pink Easter egg—or Christmas egg, if you wish—that was covered with sparkly stuff and what looked like icing, although it couldn't be eaten. When Lewis looked into the egg, he could see any battle in history. Not the battle as it really was, but as he wanted it to be. Though he didn't know it, the egg, like the balls on the tree, was capable of showing him scenes on other planets. But it was not until he was a grown-up man, working as an astronomer at Mount Palomar, that he was able to discover that property of the magic egg.

Jonathan did a lot of other things that Christmas. He put candles in all the windows of the house—electric candles, not real ones, since he liked the electric kind better—and he put strong lamps behind the stained-glass windows, so that they threw marvelous patterns of red and blue and gold and purple on the dark, sparkling snow outside. He invented the Fuse Box Dwarf, a little man who popped out at you from behind the paint cans in the cellarway and screamed, "Dreeb! Dreeb! I am the Fuse Box Dwarf!" Lewis was not scared by the little man, and he felt that those who scream, "Dreeb!" are more to be pitied than censured.

Needless to say, Jonathan put on a very good show with the coat rack mirror, though it had the habit of showing the ruins at Chichen-Itza over and over again. Somehow the mirror managed to pick up radio station WGN on its bevelled edges, so that when Lewis went out the door in the morning, he heard the Dow-Jones averages and livestock reports.

Lewis tried to enjoy himself that Christmas, but it was hard. He kept thinking that Jonathan's magic show was meant to cover up what was happening to the house. What was happening was hard to figure out, but it was strange and terrifying. After the night when Lewis saw—or dreamt he saw—Aunt Mattie, the house seemed stranger than it ever had. Sometimes the air in certain rooms seemed to shimmer as if the house was going to disappear in the next second. Sometimes the stained-glass windows showed dark and terrifying scenes, and sometimes Lewis saw in the corners of rooms those awful sights that nervous people always imagine are lurking just outside the borders of their eyesight. Walking from room to room, even in broad daylight, Lewis forgot what day it was, what he was after, and at times almost forgot who he was. At night he had dreams of wandering through the house back in the 1890's, when everything was varnished and new. Once or twice Lewis woke from such dreams to see lights flickering on his bedroom wall. They were not leaf-lights this time, but rags and patches of orange light, the kind that you see in the corners of an old house at sunset.

These strange things didn't go on all the time, of course; just now and then over the long cold winter of '48–'49. When spring came, Lewis was surprised to see that the hedge in front of the Hanchett house was wildly overgrown. It was a spiraea hedge, and had always had bristly little pink-and-white blossoms. This spring there were no blossoms on the hedge; it had turned into a dark, thorny thicket that completely hid the first floor windows and sent long waving tendrils up to scrape at the zinc gutter troughs. Burdocks and ailanthus trees had grown up overnight near the house; their branches screened the second-story windows.

Lewis still had not seen much of the new neighbor. Once, from a distance, he had caught a glimpse of a dark, huddled figure rattling a key in the front door. And from his window seat, he had seen her passing to and fro on the second floor. But, aside from that, the old woman had kept out of sight. Lewis had figured it would be like that.

She did have visitors though: one visitor. That was

Hammerhandle. Lewis had seen him coming away from Mrs. O'Meagher's back door late one night. And twice, on his way to the movies in the evening, Lewis had literally bumped into Hammerhandle, who was huddling along High Street toward the Hanchett house, his shabby overcoat buttoned up to the neck. Both times Hammerhandle had been carrying packages, odd little bundles wrapped in brown paper and twine. And both times they had collided because Hammerhandle kept looking behind him.

The second time they met this way, Hammerhandle grabbed Lewis by the collar, the way he had before. He pressed his unshaven muzzle to Lewis's ear and growled, "You little snip! You're lookin' to have your throat cut, aren't you?"

Lewis pulled away from him, but he didn't run. He faced Hammerhandle down.

"Get out of here, you rotten old bum. If you ever try to do anything to me, my uncle will fix you."

Hammerhandle laughed, though it sounded more like he was having a choking fit. "Your uncle!" he said, sneering. "Your uncle will get his sooner than he thinks! The End of the World is at hand. Don't you read your Bible like a good boy? There have been signs, and there will be more. Prepare!" And with that, he stumbled on up the hill, clutching his parcel tightly.

The day after this strange meeting was cold and rainy, and Lewis stayed indoors. Jonathan was over at Mrs.

Zimmermann's helping her bottle some prune brandy, so Lewis was alone. He decided to go poke around in the back rooms up on the third floor. The third-floor rooms were generally unused, and Jonathan had shut the heat off in them to save money. But Lewis had found interesting things up there, like boxes full of chessmen and china doorknobs and wall cupboards that you could actually climb up inside of.

Lewis wandered down the drafty hall, opening and closing doors. None of the rooms seemed worth exploring today. But wait. Sure! The room with the parlor organ. He could go play it; that would be fun.

One of the disused parlors on the third floor had a dusty old parlor organ in it. It was one of the few pieces of furniture that was left from the time Isaac Izard had lived in the house. Of course, there was the parlor organ downstairs—the good one—but it was a player organ, and often refused to let Lewis play what he wanted to play. This one up here was wheezy, and in the winter its voice was only a whisper. But you could sometimes get good tunes out of it if you pumped hard.

Lewis opened the door.

The parlor organ was a bulky shadow against one wall. Lewis found the light switch, and the light came on. He wiped some dust off the seat and sat down. What would he play? "Chopsticks," probably, or "From a Wigwam." His repertoire wasn't very large. Lewis pumped the worn treadles, and he heard a hissing and puffing that came from deep inside the machine. He touched the keys, but all he got was a gaspy tubercular sound. Darn.

He sat back and thought. Over the keys was a row of black organ stops with labels that said things like *Vox Humana*, *Salicet*, and *Flute*. Lewis knew that these stops were supposed to change the sound of the organ in various ways, but he had never pulled any of them out. Well, now was the time. He grabbed one of the black tubes and tugged gently. It wouldn't budge. He wiggled the stop and pulled harder. The whole thing came out in his hand.

Lewis sat there staring stupidly at the piece of wood. At first he felt bad about breaking the organ, but then he looked more closely at the stop. The end that had been in the organ was blunt, smooth, and painted black. There was no sign that it had ever been hooked up to anything.

What a cheesy outfit, Lewis thought. I wonder if they're all like that. Let's see. He pulled at another. *Pop!* He pulled them all out. *Pop! Pop! Pop! Pop! Pop! Pop!*

Lewis laughed. He rolled the black tubes back and forth over the keyboard. But then he stopped and thought. He had read a story once where a car had had a dummy dashboard that came out so you could hide things behind it. What if this organ . . . ?

He got up and went downstairs. He went all the way down to the cellarway, where Jonathan kept his tools. He opened the toolbox and took out a screwdriver, a hammer, and a rusty butter knife that Jonathan kept there for prying things open. Then he went back upstairs as fast as he could.

Now Lewis was sitting at the organ again. He scanned the long wooden panel; seven round black holes stared back at him. There were four screws holding the panel to the organ case, and they came out easily. Lewis stuck his fingers into two of the holes and pulled. The panel was stuck. He thought a bit, then he picked up the butter knife and slid it into a crack. *Skreek!* A little eddy of dust rose and tickled his nostrils. He moved the knife along to the right a bit and pried again. *Skreek!* The panel flopped out onto the keyboard. Ah! Now we would see what was what.

Lewis bent over and put his head close to the hole. He could smell a lot of dust, but he couldn't see a thing in there. Darn it, he had forgotten to bring a flashlight! He reached in and felt around. His arm went in all the way up to the armpit. He groped some more. What was this? Paper? He heard a dry crackling sound. Maybe it was money. He grabbed hold of the bundle and drew it out. His heart sank. It was just an old pile of papers.

Lewis sat there staring at them in disgust. So this was the secret treasure of Izard's castle! Some treasure! Well, there might be something interesting in them, like secret formulas. He flipped through the papers. Hmm . . . hmmm. . . . He flipped some more. The light in the room was very weak, and the old paper had turned practically the same shade as the copper-colored ink Isaac Izard had used. He figured the writing must be Isaac Izard's, since the first sheet said:

CLOUD FORMATIONS

AND

OTHER PHENOMENA

Observed from this Window

by

ISAAC IZARD

Hadn't Mrs. Zimmermann said that she had seen old Isaac taking notes on the sky? There were dates here and entries after them. Lewis read a few entries, and his eyes opened wider. He leafed some more.

A spatter of rain hit the window. Lewis jumped. Outside he could see thick masses of blue clouds piled up in the west. Through them ran a jagged red streak. It looked to Lewis like a hungry mouth. As he watched, the mouth opened and a ray of blood-red light shot into the room. It lit up the page he was holding. On the page were scrawled these words:

Doomsday not come yet! I'll draw it nearer by a perspective, or make a CLOCK *that shall set all the world on fire upon an instant.*

Lewis felt very frightened. He gathered the papers together and started to get up. As he did so, he heard a noise. A very faint noise. Something was fluttering around down inside the organ case.

Lewis stumbled backward, knocking over the bench. The papers slid out of his hand and scattered over the floor. What should he do? Run for his life or save the papers? He gritted his teeth and knelt down. As he gathered up the sheets, he said to himself over and over again, "*Quia tu es Deus fortitudo mea . . . quia tu es Deus fortitudo mea.*"

Now he had all the papers again. He was about to dash for the door when he saw something come floating up out of the darkness inside the organ. A moth. A moth with silver-gray wings. They shone like leaves in the moonlight.

Lewis ran to the door. He rattled the knob but he couldn't get it open. Now he could feel the moth in his hair. Lewis went rigid. His face flushed. He was not scared any more. He was angry. Very angry.

He swatted at the moth and crushed it. Lewis felt a horrible runny stickiness in his hair, and all the fear came rushing back. He wiped his hand frantically on his trouser leg. Now Lewis was out in the hall, running and shouting, "Uncle Jonathan! Mrs. Zimmermann! Come quick! Oh, please come quick, I've found something! Uncle Jonathan!"

A little while later Jonathan, Lewis, and Mrs. Zimmermann were sitting around Mrs. Zimmermann's kitchen table drinking cocoa. The dusty papers lay in a heap on

the table. Jonathan put down his mug and said, "No, Lewis. I tell you again. They're nothing to worry about. Old Isaac was crazy—crazy as a coot. This stuff has nothing to do with that ticking noise in the walls. Or if it does, it can't help us any. It can only frighten us."

"I'd say that was why Isaac left those papers there, wouldn't you, Jonathan? To frighten us to death, I mean."

This was Mrs. Zimmermann speaking. She was standing at the stove with her back to Lewis, and she was making a great show of stirring the cocoa.

"Sure. I'd say that was it, Florence," said Jonathan, nodding. "One last trick for the road and that sort of thing."

Lewis looked from one to the other. He knew they were covering up. But what could he say? One thing would lead to another, and before long he would have to tell about Halloween night. When you are hiding something, you get the feeling that every other secret is connected to your secret. Lewis couldn't challenge anyone for fear of being exposed himself.

Late that same night, Lewis lay awake in his bed listening to Jonathan and Mrs. Zimmermann talking. They were in the study below and, as usual, their voices drifted up the hot-air register. And, as usual, he couldn't quite make out what they were saying. He got out of bed and crawled over to the wooden grating in the floor. A warm breath of heat softly beat at his face. He listened. Even now, he just couldn't hear well enough. There was only one thing to do. He had to use the secret passageway.

Lewis put on his bathrobe and tiptoed down the back stairs. The kitchen was dark. Good. Slowly, carefully, he removed all the china from the shelves of the china cupboard. Then he tripped the hidden spring, and the cupboard swung outward. He walked softly in.

This time Lewis remembered to bring a flashlight. Not that he needed it much. He didn't have far to go, and light shone through many chinks into the cobwebbed passage. Before long he was standing behind the book-cases that lined the wall of Jonathan's study. He peered through a crack in the boards, and there, beyond the books, were Jonathan and Mrs. Zimmermann. Mrs. Zim-mermann had just conjured up a match out of thin air, and she was lighting a long twisted cigar with it. She blew smoke out of both corners of her mouth.

"Well, now we know," she said.

"Yes, now we know." Jonathan's voice came from his leather armchair, where he sat slumped. All that Lewis could see of him was one blue-sleeved arm and a set of hairy knuckles grasping the chair arm.

"The question is," Jonathan went on, "can we do any-thing about it?"

Mrs. Zimmermann began to pace. Cigar smoke trailed off behind her. She scraped the large purple stone of her ring along the whole length of a bookshelf. "Do?" she said. "Do? We fight them. What else?"

Jonathan gave a hoarse laugh. It made Lewis feel very uncomfortable.

"Easier said than done, Florence. They're both stronger than we are, you know. We only fiddle around with magic; they gave their lives to it. As for her, she may have quite literally given her life for it."

"But why would they want to do what they're doing?" said Mrs. Zimmermann, folding her arms and puffing angrily at her cigar. "Why? This beautiful world. End it. Why?"

Jonathan thought a minute. "Well, Florence, I can't really see into the workings of a mind like Isaac Izard's, but I'd say the answer was scientific curiosity. Think of all that's been written about the Last Day: graves opening, bodies rising up fresh and new. Some think there will be a whole new earth, much better than the present one. Wouldn't you like to see it? And another thing occurs to me. Isaac and Selenna Izard didn't enjoy this world very much. Why shouldn't they try for the next one?"

Jonathan puffed on his hookah. There was silence for several minutes.

"And the clock," said Mrs. Zimmermann. "I have to hand it to you. You were dead right. There *is* a real, literal clock in these walls. He calls it a 'device,' but it has to be a clock. He wasn't kind enough to tell us where it is, of course, though it seems to me that he tells practically everything else. He even gives hints about where he hid the key. Not that that matters now." She broke her cigar in two and threw it into the fireplace.

"But there's one thing I'd like to know," she said, turning suddenly to Jonathan. "Why did he need a clock to bring about the End of the World?"

Lewis gasped and put his hand over his mouth. Then it *was* going to be the end of the world, after all!

"Because he lost the moment," Jonathan answered. "The moment he had been seeking all those years. It was quite a search that old Isaac made. That's why he has all those crazy notes about mackerel skies and Last-Judgment skies and clouds that look like chariots and trumpets and masks of doom. That was what he was after. A mask of doom. A sky that would be right for his incantations. Sky magic is old stuff, as you know. The Romans used to——"

"Yes, yes!" cut in Mrs. Zimmermann impatiently. "I know all about sky and bird divination. Who's got the D.Mag.A. around here, anyhow? All right. So the right sky comes along for old Droopy Drawers. Fine. Dandy. So why doesn't he just wave his wand and turn us all into mullygrubs?"

"Because by the time he had made sure it was the right kind of sky, the sky had changed. It doesn't take long for clouds to move and change their patterns, you know.

Or maybe he lacked the heart to do it. It sounds silly, but I keep hoping that was what held him off."

"Him? Lack the heart? Isaac Izard? He was a hard man, Jonathan. He'd have pulled out his mother's teeth one by one, if he had to have them for some devil magic."

Jonathan sighed. "Maybe you're right. I don't know. The important thing is that he did miss his opportunity. That's why he had to build the clock. To bring the time back. The exact time when everything was right and in its place. That's what he means when he talks about 'a device to redeem the time.' Redeem, indeed! He wanted to destroy us all!"

Mrs. Zimmermann was pacing again. "All right," she said. "All right. So he built the clock. Why didn't he just wind it up?"

"He couldn't. Not all the way, at any rate. Didn't you read that passage?" Jonathan got up and went to the library table, where the papers were lying. He picked them up and leafed until he found the page he wanted.

"Ah. Here it is: 'But when the device was completed, I found that I lacked the skill to wind it all the way up. I have tried, but I must conclude that one with greater power than I possess will be needed for the final adjustment. Curse the day she left me! Curse the day she went away! *She* might have done it!' "

Jonathan looked up. "In that last sentence the word 'she' is underlined four times. 'She,' of course, is our friend across the street."

Lewis closed his eyes. Mrs. O'Meagher really was Mrs. Izard then! He had guessed it, of course, but he hadn't been sure. Mrs. Izard! And he had let her out. He felt like the stupidest, most foolish person in the whole world.

"Ah, yes," said Mrs. Zimmermann, smiling wryly. "Well, we shall see in the end who is stronger. But tell me one thing more, oh, sage, since it seems that you have been cast in the role of explicator and annotator of the testament of Isaac Izard."

"Yes? What would you like to know, Florence?"

"Well, he claims that the clock isn't wound all the way up. But it has been making a ticking sound for years now. A magic ticking that seems to be coming from behind every wall of this house. It's hard for me to believe that the clock is just whiling the time away until old Auntie Izard arrives with her key. *What is the clock doing?*"

Jonathan shrugged. "Search me, Florence. Maybe it's trying to drag the house back into the past without the aid of that 'final adjustment.' Maybe he fixed it so the ticking sound would scare away anyone who might be foolish enough to come and live in this house. Isaac didn't want his clock found by accident and destroyed, after all. I don't know why the clock is ticking, Florence. But I do know this. When Mrs. Izard or whoever is over there puts that key in the slot of that clock and finishes the job that Isaac started, then—at that moment—Isaac

Izard will return. You and I and Lewis will be ghosts or something worse, and he will be standing in the turret with power in his right hand. And the End of the World will come to pass."

Lewis clamped both hands over his mouth. He fell to his knees, shuddering and sobbing. For a moment he was on the verge of shouting, "Here I am! Come and get me!" so they could come and take him away and put him in the Detention Home for life. But he didn't shout. He clamped his hands more tightly over his mouth and cried in muffled bursts that shook his whole body. He cried for a long time, and when he was through, he sat staring listlessly at the dark wall of the passageway.

Mrs. Zimmermann and Jonathan left the room. The fire burned low, but still Lewis sat there. His mouth was full of the taste of ammonia, and his eyes burned. He took his handkerchief out of the pocket of his bathrobe and blew his nose. Where was the flashlight? Ah. Here it was. He clicked it on.

Lewis got up slowly and started to pick his way toward the entrance. Even though he was walking upright, he felt as if he were slinking. Now he was running his hand over the splintery back of the china cupboard. He tripped the spring, and the cupboard swung silently outward. Lewis half expected to see Mrs. Zimmermann and Jonathan sitting there with their arms folded, waiting for him. But the kitchen was dark and empty.

Lewis went up to his room. He felt as if he had stayed awake three nights in a row. Without even stopping to take off his bathrobe, he threw himself onto the rumpled bed. Darkness filled his brain, and he fell into a dead dreamless sleep.

CHAPTER NINE

The next day was Saturday, and Lewis woke up in a state of panic. He was like a pressure cooker with the lid clamped on tight and the steam hole clogged up with chewing gum. Thoughts kept bubbling and seething to the surface of his mind, but none of them seemed to make sense. What was he going to do? What *could* he do?

Lewis sat up and looked around the room. Two long panes of sunlight lay on the splintered and paint-stained floor. Over by the fireplace stood a tall mirror with battlements on top that matched the ones on Lewis's bed. Before the mirror lay a beautiful hooked rug. Jonathan claimed that Mrs. Zimmermann's great-grandmother had made it. The pattern of the rug was "Autumn Leaves."

Scallop-edged leaves, bright gold and deep blood-red, with some green ones thrown in for contrast. The rug seemed to float before the mirror, and the leaves swam in the pool of bright sunlight. It was an illusion, of course. This was no magic carpet. But Lewis liked to stand on it in the morning while he was dressing. It made him feel that he was free of the earth, if only for a little while.

He stood on it now as he pulled on his pants and tucked in his shirt. The shimmer of leaves lifted him off the floor. Things seemed clearer now. He had to get hold of Tarby. Tarby would know what to do. It was true that he had been avoiding Lewis, but they weren't exactly enemies. And anyway, Tarby was in this thing as deep as he was. He had held the flashlight while Lewis drew the magic pentacle and chalked in the name, Selenna. That must be Mrs. Izard's first name, Lewis thought. She must have put it in my head. Then, behind those iron doors, she was never really dead. . . .

Lewis bit his lip to cut off this line of thought. He went downstairs, ate breakfast alone, and hurried out the door. Tarby, with his nine brothers and sisters, lived in a huge frame house halfway across town. Lewis had never been invited there and he did not even know the first names of Tarby's mother and father, let alone the names of any of the nine brothers and sisters. He knew that Mr. Corrigan—that was Tarby's last name—ran a hardware store. And that was about all Lewis knew.

It was a bright, windy April day, and the sky was full

of little white clouds that kept tearing apart and merging into each other. Birds were flying about and the lawns were showing that first livid wet green. When Lewis got to the Corrigan house he found a bunch of small children playing in the front yard, which was all chewed up and full of mud holes. One of the younger ones, who looked a lot like Tarby, was hanging by his knees from one of the limbs of a dead tree that had red taillight reflectors nailed all over it. Other kids were making mud castles, beating each other over the head with sand shovels, trying to ride broken tricycles, or just sitting around screaming at the top of their lungs. Lewis picked his way past the toy trucks and inner tubes that littered the front walk. He pushed the doorbell and waited.

After a while a fat, tired-looking woman came to the door. She had a baby in her arms, and it was batting her on the shoulder with a bottle that it held by the nipple.

"Yes?" She sounded crabby, and no wonder.

"Uh . . . Mrs. Corrigan? I wonder if you could tell me where Tarby is."

"Tarby? Gee, I wonder if he's in the house. I'll see."

She threw back her head and bellowed, "Taaar-beeee!" No answer, though it would have been hard to hear one over the racket.

"No, I guess not," she said. She smiled a tired, kind smile. "He's probably out playing ball with the other kids."

Lewis thanked her and was about to turn away when she said, "Say! Aren't you that Barnavelt boy?"

Lewis said that he was.

She gave him a pleading look. "Please don't tell Tarby any more stories about ghosts and graveyards. He had nightmares for a week after last Halloween. It was nice of your uncle to invite him over for a cider-and-doughnut party, and let him stay the night and all, but those stories . . . well, you know how sensitive he is."

Lewis managed to keep a straight face. "Mm . . . sure . . . okay, Mrs. Corrigan, I won't tell him any more ghost stories. See you."

As he picked his way back down the walk, tripping on toys and dodging one or two mud balls that were thrown his way, Lewis had a hard time keeping from laughing right out loud. So that was Tarby's version of last Halloween night! Well, well. And where had Tarby spent the night? Shuddering under the back porch? Sleeping in a tree? And a whole week of nightmares! Of course, he hadn't been scared. It was just the moonlight. Lewis's inner laughter turned into a wry grin.

Lewis stopped at a hitching block to tie his shoelace. Now what was he going to do? Well, there were only two regular baseball diamonds in New Zebedee. The one out behind the school, and the one at the athletic field. He decided to go to the one behind the school.

When he got there, he found Tarby playing ball with

a lot of other kids. He was pitching, and various boys were shouting, "Come on, Tar-babee! Strike him out!" and, "Give 'em the old knuckleball!" or, if they happened to be on the other side, "Yaah! Pitcher's got a rubber arm!"

Tarby wound up with a windmill motion, balked several times—this was allowed, because it was softball, not baseball—and when he had the batter making nervous little half-swings, he fired the ball up to the plate. The batter swung so hard that he fell down.

"Strrrike three! Yerrr—out!" yelled the boy who was the umpire.

Lewis, standing on the sidelines, cupped his hands to his mouth and shouted, "Hey, Tarby! Can I talk to you?"

"Not now, Fatty. I'm in the middle of a game."

Tears filled Lewis's eyes. Tarby had never called him "fatty" before. At least he couldn't remember him doing it. Lewis choked back the tears and stood waiting patiently while Tarby mowed down the next batter with three blazing fastballs. That was the third out, so Tarby's team came in from the field. Carelessly, Tarby threw his glove on the ground and said, "Hi, Lewis. C'n I do f'ya?"

"My Uncle Jonathan's in some awful trouble. We're all in awful trouble. You know that night when we went up to the cemetery?"

To Lewis's complete surprise, Tarby grabbed him

by the collar and yanked him forward till their faces were about two inches apart.

"Look. If they ever find out that you were up there that night, you tell them that you were there by yourself. If you don't, you'll have two broken arms and maybe a broken head."

Lewis tried to shake himself free of Tarby's grip, but he couldn't. He felt blood rushing into his face as he shouted, "Tarby, this is worse than Halloween stuff! This is ghosts and witches and devils and . . . *let go of me, you candle-head!*"

Tarby let go of Lewis. He stared at him with his mouth open. "Candle-head" was just a name someone had called someone in a comic book Lewis was reading. It didn't mean anything.

Tarby's lips drew together. "What did you call me?"

Several of the other boys started to shout, "Fight! Fight!" though they really didn't expect much of one. It was only Lewis, after all.

Lewis stood there red-faced and frightened.

"I . . . I don't know what I called you."

"Well, remember next time." Tarby raised his fist and brought it down hard on Lewis's shoulder. It really hurt.

"C'mon, Tarby," shouted a tall boy named Carl Holabaugh. "Don't waste your time with Tubbo. You lead off this inning, and we're six runs behind. Get up there and slug it."

Tarby turned back to the game, and Lewis stumbled

off down the street, rubbing his shoulder. He was crying.

With the tears still welling uncontrollably into his eyes, Lewis started to walk. He walked all over town, past rows of houses that stared at him blankly. They had no advice to give him. He walked down Main Street, and stared for a while at the Civil War Monument. But the stone soldiers with their upraised bayonets and cannon swabbers did not have anything to say to him, either. He walked to the other end of Main Street and stared at the fountain that spumed a crystal willow tree from within a circle of marble columns. At night the fountain was lit up and it turned from red to orange and from orange to yellow and from yellow to blue and from blue to green and back to red again. But right now it was clear. Lewis wished his mind were clear too, but it wasn't.

He walked around the fountain three or four times, and then he crossed the street and started to walk up U.S. 9, which took up where Main Street left off, and led out of town. When he got to the square, tin CITY LIMITS sign, he just walked off into some tall grass and sat there, watching the ants crawl and listening to the cars as they whooshed past. His eyes were dry now. He was through crying. It occurred to him that he had been doing a lot of crying lately. That wasn't going to solve anything. Thinking might help, though he wasn't sure it would. He sat and thought, and tried to make up his mind what to do.

It was late in the afternoon when Lewis got up. He almost fell over because his left leg had gone to sleep. After he had stomped around in the weeds for a while to get the circulation going again, he set out for home. His mind was made up. All he could hear in his head was the old church hymn that ran:

> Once to every man and nation
> Comes the moment to decide
> In the strife of truth with falsehood
> For the good or evil side.

He imagined that he was leading a cavalry charge. If he had had one of Jonathan's canes with him, he would have swung it like a sword. Now and then he stopped and felt goose-pimple shivers run in waves through his body. He felt very proud and brave, and very frightened too. It is a hard thing to describe.

That night, long after everyone had gone to sleep, Lewis crawled out of bed and tiptoed down the front stairs. The house was quiet, very quiet, because it was one of those nights when Jonathan had stopped all the clocks —all but the one he couldn't stop. Out in the front hall the mirror on the coat rack was talking to itself amid little bursts of static. Now and then its edges flickered faintly. Maybe it was trying to warn Lewis. If it was, he ignored the warning. His mind was made up. He had started this whole horrible business, and now he was going to try to end it.

His hand rested on the cool lip of the Willoware umbrella stand. He groped among the canes, rattling them a good deal. Ah, here it was. His hand closed on the black wooden rod and—what was this? Lewis pulled his fingers away with a sucked-in gasp. Touching the magic cane was like touching a living human arm. Life pulsed through it. Lewis stood there staring at the cane. Its globe was now faintly lit. In the gray light he saw snow swirling, and there, shadowy but real, was the strange little castle. The magic light cast a pale shaking blotch on the wallpaper. Could he use it, this thing of power? It occurred to him that Jonathan was being very modest when he called himself a parlor magician.

Lewis set his teeth and reached out with a hand that still tingled from the shock it had received. He grasped the rod firmly. He drew it out. The globe sizzled and crackled, and turned from gray to rosy pink and then back to gray again. Now he opened the front door. A wet fresh-smelling breeze blew in and banged the door gently against the wall. The leaves of the chestnut tree drifted and sighed, and white blossoms came sailing down. He looked across the street. Despite the overgrown hedge, he could see that there were lights on in the Hanchett house. Muttering a prayer, he started down the steps.

In the middle of the street he almost turned and ran, but something kept him going. Once he had crossed to the other side it seemed easier to go on. It was like running downhill with the wind pushing you. The hedge parted at the brick walk that led up to the front stoop. Lewis walked in under the overhanging branches. Now he was at the bottom of the steps.

The Hanchett house had an old-fashioned double door of black wood with two frosted panes set in it. The panes had always reminded Lewis of the Ten Commandments, and now he thought: *Thou shalt not enter.* But one door panel stood ajar. Was he expected? His heart was pounding, but he went up.

He stopped just inside the door, under the hall lamp. The corridor was empty. Empty and bare. There wasn't a stick of furniture in it, no chairs or chests or little tables. No umbrellas propped against walls. On the pale, rose-colored wallpaper Lewis saw dark squares. The squares were the color the paper had been when it was new. The Hanchetts had hung pictures in these spaces, but now the pictures were gone. Mrs. O'Meagher had not put up any of her own.

Lewis walked quietly to the wide arch that opened into the living room. No one there. Some furniture, but not much. A few weak-looking little chairs with bow legs and an uncomfortable-looking couch. One low coffee table with two postage-stamp-sized china ash trays. One blow from Jonathan's flat-bottomed pipe would have smashed either one to smithereens. Lewis went from chair to chair, touching polished arms and smooth upholstered backs. He half expected the furniture to pop, like soap bubbles, when he touched it. But everything was solid. The floor was so highly polished that you could see your reflection in it. Over on one wall was a brick fireplace. It was painted bright pink all over, even on its inside walls. There were no soot stains. Apparently the old witch didn't like fires. Two birch logs were balanced neatly on the shiny brass andirons.

On the mantelpiece Lewis saw something that surprised him: an ornament. It was one of those whirligigs with tin cutout angels. You lit the candles in the middle, and the heat made the angels go around. These angels were blowing trumpets. Lewis reached up and touched the little wheel. *Squeee.* It spun tipsily. The sound startled him so much that he whirled around, holding the magic cane up for protection. No one was there.

He looked in the kitchen. A couple of little plaster plaques on the wall and an electric clock. A red formica counter and a tubular steel chair, also upholstered in cherry red. In the corner there was an icebox. He opened it and found one bottle of Coke. Or was it Coke? He turned the bottle over in his hands. It was gritty on the outside. Covered with dirt. Like it had been buried. And the liquid inside—it was lighter than Coke. Sort of a brownish red. Lewis put the bottle back. He shut the icebox door. The house seemed to be filled with a humming noise, and he knew that it was his blood in his ears. Gripping the magic cane with a trembling, sweaty hand, he went to inspect the other rooms.

He checked out the whole first floor, but he found

nothing—nothing but more half-furnished rooms. A chair here, a table there. What lamps there were, were unplugged, but a bare ceiling fixture burned in each room. Now Lewis was at the bottom of the brightly lit staircase. He paused for a moment and then, suddenly, he pounded the cane on the floor and shouted, "I have come to defeat you, Mrs. Izard! Show yourself! Are you afraid of me? You ought to be! I know who you are and what you want to do. I challenge you to a duel by the ancient rules of magic!"

Lewis had expected his challenge to sound grand and majestic, to ring high and clear like a blast on a silver trumpet. Instead, it fell flat. It died away in the heavy stillness of the house. Lewis felt foolish. His cheeks burned. And he began to get worried.

Lewis did not know a blessed thing about "the ancient rules of magic." He had come over here with Jonathan's magic stick in his hand, hoping that the stick would do his work for him. Now he was doubtful. What if the cane wouldn't work for anyone but its master? What if Mrs. Izard's magic was stronger than Jonathan's?

Lewis looked at the burning globe, and he looked up the staircase. He felt like turning around and running home as fast as he could. But then how would he save Mrs. Zimmermann and Jonathan and the world, and make up for what he had done?

The house was very silent. Lewis took a deep breath and started to climb the staircase.

Halfway up the stairs, on the broad landing, Lewis stopped to look at a picture. It was the only picture he had seen in the house. There, in a heavy oval black frame, was a photo of an unpleasant-looking old man. He was sitting or standing—you couldn't tell which—against a wall covered with intricately patterned wallpaper. Lewis looked at the picture for a long time. He took in all the details: the two or three strands of hair combed over the almost-bald head, the deep-set eyes that seemed to be staring right at him, the hawkish nose. He looked at the man's clothing. He was wearing an old-fashioned, stiff cardboard collar with folded-back points. And his left hand rested on the ball of what must be a cane. There appeared to be some writing on the cane, but Lewis couldn't read it.

Lewis stood there wondering who the old man was. Could it be . . . ? He snatched the picture down and looked on the back. No label. Quickly he turned it over and stared at the picture again. Something was familiar. Of course! The wallpaper! It was the wallpaper in the upstairs front hallway. Roman numeral II's hooked together with curlicues. Lewis knew now that he was staring at a picture of Isaac Izard.

Then it was all true. This woman was his wife, come back from the grave to . . . to do what? Lewis felt his heart pounding. He was more scared than he had ever been in his life. He didn't want to fight Mrs. Izard any more. He just wanted to get out. He looked frantically up the stairs toward the dark doorway of the bedroom. No one was coming. He started down the stairs, but Mrs. Izard was in the way.

She stood there smiling. In her hand was an ivory-handled cane. "Well, young man, what is it? What makes you think you can roam around other people's houses at night? What do you want?"

Lewis was afraid he might faint, but he didn't. Instead, he felt himself stiffen. He raised the cane. "I don't know what you want to do to us, Mrs. Izard," he said, "but you're not going to do it. My uncle's magic is stronger than yours."

She laughed a harsh, nasty laugh. "Do you mean that toy cane? He probably got it at the Capharnaum County Fair. Don't be foolish, child."

All through the house the cane had burned with a steady gray light. Now, as Mrs. Izard spoke, the globe began to go dark. Lewis looked down and saw that he was staring at something that looked very much like a burned-out light bulb.

"And now," said Mrs. Izard, stepping forward, "and now, my fine young friend, you will see what it is to bother nice old ladies who just want to be left alone."

She snatched the cane from his numb hand and threw it clattering down the stairs. Now she was bending over him, and the light reflected from her spectacles hurt his eyes. Her voice was angry now, and she talked faster.

"Do you have any idea what it is like to be buried

deep in the earth, dark stone all around, no one to hear you or see you, your only company a dead man? *Do you?*"

"Stop right there, Mrs. Izard. You're not dealing with children now."

There at the bottom of the stairs stood Mrs. Zimmermann. Her face was lit by invisible footlights, and she wore a floor-length purple cape. In the folds, instead of shadows, were deep wells of orange fire. In one hand she held a tall black pole with a clear glass globe on top. Inside the globe a magenta star burned. It grew in brightness when she spoke and dwindled when she was silent.

Mrs. Izard turned around. She faced Mrs. Zimmermann calmly. "So it's you," she said. "Well, my power has not reached its height, but I am still strong enough to deal with you. *Aroint ye!*"

She pointed the ivory cane at Mrs. Zimmermann. Nothing happened. She stopped smiling and dropped her cane.

Now it was Mrs. Zimmermann's turn. She pounded the butt of her staff once on the floor, and the staircase was lit with a flash of ultraviolet lightning. With an awful scraping cry that no human ever made, Mrs. Izard rushed past Lewis and up the stairs. Mrs. Zimmermann started up after her.

"Run back home, Lewis!" she shouted as she dashed past him. "You're a brave boy, but you're no match for that thing. *Run,* I tell you!"

Lewis bounded down the stairs, taking them two at a time. He was terrified, but he was very happy too. As he ran down the front steps of the house he heard strange exploding sounds and sharp cries. Branches grabbed at him as he ran along the well-swept brick walk. One of them actually wrapped itself around his left leg and started to pull. With a scream and a frantic thrashing motion, Lewis tore loose and plunged across the street. He threw open the gate and ran *whump!* into something hard and yet soft. Jonathan.

Lewis broke down. He began to weep hysterically with his face pressed into Jonathan's blue work shirt. Jonathan wrapped his arms around Lewis and held him tight. Though Lewis could not see it, Jonathan was staring over his head at the Hanchett house, and there was a grim smile on his face. A purple flash lit up one of the upstairs windows. Now a cold, blue-white pinpoint was kindled in the adjoining window, as if someone had just lit a strange kind of match. The blue light spread till it filled the window. It spread to the other window and ate up the fading purple light. Now there was a dull powerful explosion like an aerial bomb at a fireworks display. It hurt Jonathan's ears. As he watched, both upstairs windows turned a brilliant purple. The chimney of the house toppled, and its bricks slid down the roof. The overgrown hedge thrashed and swayed as if it had been caught in a hurricane. Several diamond-shaped pieces of glass fell out of their frames and tinkled on the walk below. Then the house was silent and dark.

Lewis had stopped crying, and now he turned around to look. A full minute passed. Then the front door scraped open and Mrs. Zimmermann appeared. She walked calmly down the steps and down the brick walk and out into the street, humming as she went. The orange fires in the creases of her robe had gone out, and so had the magic footlights. In one hand she held an old umbrella. The handle of the umbrella was a crystal knob, and a tiny seed of violet fire still burned in it. In her other hand Mrs. Zimmermann held Jonathan's cane; its globe was still dark.

"Hi, Florence," said Jonathan, as if he were meeting her on the street on a Sunday afternoon. "How did it go?"

"Well enough," she said, handing him his cane. "Here's your magic wand. It's had quite a shock, but I think it'll recover. As for Mrs. Izard, I just don't know. I may have destroyed her, or I may have just put her out of action for a while. In any case, let's take the time that has been given to us and *find that clock!*"

CHAPTER TEN

When the three of them got back to the house, they had a shock. The ticking was very loud now, louder than it had ever been. It was like standing inside the works of Big Ben.

Jonathan turned pale. "It looks," he said, "as if things are drawing to some conclusion. Mrs. Izard may not be as dead as we could wish."

Mrs. Zimmermann began to pace back and forth. She rubbed the purple stone of her ring against her chin. "She may be, or she may not be. Either way, having her out of the way is no guarantee that the bomb won't blow up in our faces," she said. "But let's assume the worst. Let's assume that she's still in the game. All right." She took a deep breath and let it out. "It has been my theory, ever since yesterday, that the old hag is just waiting for the proper *time* to use that wretched key. The proper action at the proper time to achieve the proper effect. That would be like her. And like her old husband too. His magic is logical. It proceeds from A to B to C in nice, neat steps. As logical and neat as the movement of a hand around the face of a clock."

"Then there's no point in our being logical, is there?" said Jonathan. He was smiling very strangely and clicking the paper clips on his watch chain. This was always a sign that he was thinking.

"What do you mean?" said Lewis and Mrs. Zimmermann at the same time.

"I mean," he said patiently, "that we're no good at that sort of game. Our game is wild swoops, sudden inexplicable discoveries, cloudy thinking. Knights' jumps instead of files of rooks plowing across the board. So we'd better play our way if we expect to win."

Mrs. Zimmermann folded her arms and looked grumpy. "I see," she said. "It sounds very reasonable. If you're in a chess game, draw to an inside straight. If you're playing tennis, try to hit a home run. Very intelligent."

Jonathan seemed unruffled. "Why not?" he said. "It all seems clear enough to me. Lewis, what I want you to do is this. Get a pencil and paper, and dream up the silliest set of instructions you can think of."

Lewis looked puzzled. "Instructions for what?"

"For a ceremony. A ritual. A magic show for getting the clock out of its hiding place. Make it as goofy as you can."

Lewis felt very excited and happy. "Okay," he said. "If that's what you want, here we go!"

He ran to the sideboard and dug out a yellow Ticonderoga NO. 2 pencil and a five-cent pad of writing paper. Then he ran into the study and slammed the doors. Jonathan and Mrs. Zimmermann paced nervously outside, and the gigantic ticking continued.

Fifteen minutes later Lewis slid back the doors of the study. He handed Jonathan a blue-lined sheet of paper with writing on both sides. The first line that Jonathan read made him throw back his head and laugh loudly. He mumbled rapidly through the rest of the list, chuckling all the while. Mrs. Zimmermann kept trying to read it over his shoulder, but finally she lost her temper and snatched it out of his hand. She laughed even harder than Jonathan had. She snortled and cackled and giggled. Finally, she handed the paper back to Jonathan.

"Okay," she said. "So be it. First we put lighted candles in all the windows. Real candles, that is."

"Yes," said Jonathan, wrinkling up his nose. "I see Lewis has the poor taste to prefer real candles. Ah, well . . . let's get going. There are several boxes of candle ends in the sideboard."

Jonathan took the first floor, Mrs. Zimmermann took

the second floor, and Lewis took the third floor and the stained-glass windows, wherever they might be. Before long, the whole house was lit up for Christmas in April.

Lewis paused outside the door of the room that had Isaac Izard's organ in it. He looked into the shoe box that had been full of candle stubs. Only one left. Should he put it in there? No, there was a better place.

With a fat red candle in his hand, Lewis climbed the dusty spiral staircase that led to the cupola room. He shoved open the narrow door. The room was dark except for streaks of moonlight on the floor. Lewis moved over to the window. He knelt down and leaned forward into the deep embrasure.

The oval window gave him a bird's-eye view of the Hanchett house. Or would have, if he had been able to see it. Brilliant moonlight bathed the hill, but the Hanchett house lay in a mass of shadow. Only the dark point of its roof could be seen.

Lewis stared, fascinated. Then, suddenly, he began to hear the ticking, faint but audible, that filled even this room in the house at 100 High Street. He shook his head, got out his matches, and quickly lit the candle.

When he got back downstairs, he found that his second instruction was being obeyed. Mrs. Zimmermann was playing "Chopsticks" on the organ in the front parlor. When she got up and went back to the dining room, the organ kept on playing "Chopsticks," since it was a player organ, and she had set it on "Infinite Replay." The silly monotonous music almost drowned out the steady ticking—almost, but not quite.

Jonathan came bouncing in from the back bedrooms. His face was red, and he was breathing hard. "Okay," he said. "What's next?"

Mrs. Zimmermann picked up the paper and read in a solemn voice. "We are to play a game of Bon-Sour-One-Frank until the Ace of Nitwits appears."

As unlikely as it may seem, Jonathan knew what Bon-Sour-One-Frank was. It was Lewis's name for poker. The three of them had played a lot of poker since that first August evening, and Lewis had named the game for the inscription he thought he saw on the shiny brass one-franc pieces. When you called someone, you had to shout, "Bon Sour One Frank!" very loudly.

But Jonathan was puzzled about one detail. He turned to Lewis with a quizzical look on his face. "And what, may I ask, is the Ace of Nitwits?"

"I don't know. It just came to me. I guess we'll know when we find it."

Out came the red box of coins. Out came the blue and gold cards. Jonathan lit his pipe and unbuttoned his vest till it was only held together by the chain of paper clips. He got his dusty old gray fedora out of the closet and parked it on the back of his head. This, he explained, was the proper poker-playing costume.

Jonathan shuffled and dealt. Shekels and guilders, ducats and florins, drachmas and didrachmas clattered over the table. At first the hands were ordinary. Pair of eights, nothing, kings and tens. Then people started getting six of a kind and cards with square-root signs and question marks all over them. Jonathan and Mrs. Zimmermann were not pulling any tricks. The strange cards appeared all by themselves. On they played, while the giant clock ticked and the organ played "Chopsticks" and the candles threw fruit and flower patterns or plain yellow splotches onto the gray moonlit grass outside.

It was after a half hour of playing that Lewis picked up a card and found that he was staring at the Ace of Nitwits. There it was. Instead of clubs or hearts, it had ears of corn and green peppers all over it. In the center was a dopey-looking man in a flat black hat called a mortarboard, the kind of hat that college professors wear to graduations. Ice cream was heaped up on the hat, and the professor was tasting it with his index finger.

Lewis showed the card around.

"Why so it is!" cried Jonathan. "The Ace of Nitwits! I'd recognize it anywhere. Now just what does *that* mean, Lewis?"

"It means you have to wear it stuck to your forehead with a piece of bubble gum. Here." Lewis took out the piece he had been chewing and handed it to Uncle Jonathan.

"Thanks awfully," said Jonathan. He squashed the card against his forehead. "Now what?"

"You get all done up and come down with the eight ball, like it says in the instructions."

"Hm. Yes. Righty-ho, and all that sort of thing. See you, folks."

Jonathan went upstairs. He stayed up there a long time, so long that the parlor organ broke into "Stars and Stripes Forever" out of pure boredom. Mrs. Zimmermann sat tapping her fingers on the table, while Lewis did what he always did when he was nervously waiting for somebody. He slapped the sides of his chair, rocked back and forth, and wiggled his right leg.

"Well, here I am!"

Mrs. Zimmermann and Lewis looked up. There at the head of the stairs stood Jonathan. He was wearing a cape made from a crazy quilt, and on his head was a flowered toaster cover Mrs. Zimmermann had made. The Ace of Nitwits was still glued to his forehead, and he bore in his hands a small, round, black object. As he started down the stairs, the organ played "Pomp and Circumstance," but it soon got tired of that and switched to radio commercials:

> Call for Cuticura
> It's fragrant, and pura
> It's mildly medicated too
> It's grand for you and yoo-hooo!

> Clark's Super One Hundred Gasoline
> Thousands say it's best!
> The largest-selling, independent gasoline
> In the Middle West!
>
> Super Suds, Super Suds
> Lots more suds from Super Su-u-uds
> Richer longer lasting too
> They're the ones with Super Doo-oo-oooo.

To this solemn accompaniment, Jonathan advanced to the dining-room table and set down the black ball. It was one of those fortune-telling eight-balls, the kind you buy in dime stores. The ball was full of fluid, and when you shook it, ghostly white cards came floating up to the little window. There were only three of them: YES, NO, and MAYBE.

"Now what?" asked Jonathan.

"Ask it," said Lewis.

"Ask it what?" Jonathan looked blank.

"The circumference of the moon, you bearded booby!" screamed Mrs. Zimmermann. "Where I left my hat after the Chicago World's Fair! Now *think* a minute, Jonathan. What would you *want* to ask it?"

"Where the clock is?" asked Jonathan in a small voice.

A burst of rather mechanical applause came from the front room. It was the organ, smarting off as usual. Jonathan stuck his tongue out at it over his shoulder. Then he turned back to the table where the eight-ball lay.

Carefully, reverently, he picked it up. He held it like a microphone and talked into it.

"Where is the clock?"

The dark window stayed dark. Jonathan shook the ball till the liquid inside it foamed. *"Where is the clock?"* he shouted, and he repeated this question in Greek, Latin, French, German, and Middle-Kingdom Egyptian. Still no answer.

"Your French is terrible," said Mrs. Zimmermann, grabbing the ball out of his hand. "Here . . . let me try."

Holding the ball under a corner of her cloak as if she were protecting it from rain, Mrs. Zimmermann jabbered at it in Bengali, Finno-Ugric, Basque, Old High Norse, and Geez. She used all the commands for unlocking the secrets of specular stones that are favored by Regiomontanus, Albertus Magnus, and Count Cagliostro. Still nothing.

"Can I try?" asked Lewis. His voice was timid and weak.

Mrs. Zimmermann looked down at him. Perspiration was pouring along all the wrinkles of her face. Her eyes looked wild. "What did you say?"

"I wonder if I might try. I know I'm not a wizard or anything, but it *is* my ball. I bought it in Chicago and . . ."

"Of course!" cried Mrs. Zimmermann, pounding the table with her fist. "Of *course!* What fools we are! Like any magic object, it only responds to its owner. Here. But hurry!" She shoved the ball into his hands.

The ticking of the clock got softer, but it was faster now.

Lewis held the magic toy up before his face. His voice was calm and quiet. "Please tell us where the clock is," he whispered.

There was motion inside the ball. YES drifted out of the void like a ghostly newspaper in a black wind. It passed by. So did NO and MAYBE. Finally, after several tense minutes, a card appeared bearing the words: COAL PIT.

"It says coal pit." Lewis's voice was dull and lifeless now. He hung his head.

"May I see the ball?" said Jonathan softly. Lewis handed it to him.

Jonathan held the ball up to the light. He wrinkled his forehead, and the Ace of Nitwits fluttered away to the floor. "Yes, it certainly says 'coal pit.' Coal pit? *Coal pit?* What the devil does it mean by saying *that?*" Jonathan glowered at the shiny little ball. He was beginning to think it might be nice to dash the wretched thing against the mantelpiece.

Suddenly the ball hiccuped. Jonathan glanced quickly down at it, and saw that the little window was filled with bubbles.

"Oh, good grief! Look at this, Florence. Now it thinks it's a Bendix washer. Shall we get out the ouija board?"

"Wait a minute," said Mrs. Zimmermann. "It looks like the bubbles are starting to break up."

Lewis, Jonathan, and Mrs. Zimmermann watched breathlessly as the little bubbles popped, one by one. Pop, pop, pop. It seemed to take forever. Meanwhile, the clock ticked.

At last the window was clear. Now the sign said: COAL BIN.

"Oh, great!" said Jonathan. "Just great! Now it says coal *bin!* That's a big improvement."

"Don't you have a coal bin?" asked Mrs. Zimmermann.

Jonathan gave her an irritated look. "Of course not, Florence! You ought to know that. Remember, I switched to oil when I bought this . . . oh! *Oh!*" Jonathan clapped his hands over his mouth. "Oh! I think I see! Come on, everybody. We're going to the basement."

Lewis and Mrs. Zimmermann followed Jonathan to the kitchen. He opened the cellar door, and jumped back as if he had been hit in the face. The ticking down there was thunderous.

Jonathan looked at Mrs. Zimmermann. His face was haggard, and his eyes were wide with fear. "Got your umbrella, Florence? Good. Then down we go."

Over in a black sooty corner of the basement was the old coal bin. Two of its walls were formed by gray slats nailed to worm-eaten wooden pillars. The other two walls were whitewashed stone, and up against one of these lay a high rampart of coal. It had been there when Jonathan moved in, and he had always meant to have it hauled away.

"I certainly get the idiot prize," he said quietly. Jonathan took a long backswing and started shoveling. Lewis and Mrs. Zimmermann helped with their hands. Before long they had cleared all the coal away from the wall.

"Doesn't *look* like there's any secret panel," said Jonathan, feeling around for springs and hidden levers. "But then, if it looked that way, it wouldn't be secret, would it? Hmm . . . no . . . nothing. I'm afraid we'll have to use the pick. Stand back, everybody."

Lewis and Mrs. Zimmermann got well away from the wall, and Jonathan started swinging. By now the ticking was hurried and staccato, and the blows of the pick were like heavy beats in the rhythm. Every stroke sent whitish-gray chips flying in all directions. But it was an easier job than anyone would have thought. The wall began to shake and crumble at Jonathan's first stroke, and the whole solid-looking mass was soon lying in pieces on the hard dirt floor of the cellar. For it had not been a real wall, but merely a plaster mock-up. What lay behind was a weathered, old wooden door with a black china knob. There was a lock plate, but there was no keyhole.

Jonathan leaned his pick up against a pillar and stepped back.

"Don't dawdle!" said Mrs. Zimmermann nervously. "Get that door open! I have a feeling that we are on the very edge of disaster."

Jonathan stood there rubbing his chin. Exasperated, Mrs. Zimmermann grabbed his arm and started to shake it. "Hurry, Jonathan! What on earth are you waiting for?"

"I'm trying to think of door-opening spells. Know any?"

"Why not pull at it?" said Lewis. "It may not be locked."

Jonathan was about to say that he had never heard of anything so stupid in all his life. But he never got a chance to say this. The door opened all by itself.

Jonathan, Mrs. Zimmermann, and Lewis stared. They were looking down a long corridor—more like a mine shaft it was, really, with square wooden arches diminishing into the dark distance. Something vague and gray was moving at the far end of the tunnel. It seemed to be getting closer.

"Look!" cried Lewis.

He was not pointing at the gray shape. He was pointing at something that was sitting on the floor of the tunnel, right there at their feet.

A clock. A plain, old, Waterbury eight-day clock.

Its pendulum oscillated madly behind a little glass door, and it was making a sound like a Geiger counter gone crazy.

"I'm so glad you've done my work for me," said a voice behind them. Jonathan and Mrs. Zimmermann spun around and froze. Really froze. They could not move their hands or feet or heads. They couldn't even wiggle their ears. They were completely paralyzed, though they could still see and hear.

There stood Mrs. Izard. Or Mrs. O'Meagher, or whatever name you choose. She was wearing a black-velvet cloak with an ivory brooch at her neck. The brooch bore a raised Greek omega. In her right hand was a plain black rod, and in her left she carried what looked like a severed hand with a lighted candle growing out of its back. Concentric rings of yellow light spread outward from the hand, and through them Jonathan and Mrs. Zimmermann could see Mrs. Izard's glasses, which looked like tablets of gray slate.

"I do hope you haven't tired yourselves, my dears," said the old woman in a nasty, sneering voice. "I do hope you haven't. But if you have, it's all been in a good cause. I couldn't have done anything without you. Not a thing. Because, you see, since I was set free, I've been able to pass through walls and doors, but these poor old hands of mine just haven't been able to wield tools. I even had to get Mr. Hammerhandle to find this for me."

She let go of her wand—it stood up by itself—and reached deep into the folds of her cloak. What she brought out was a greenish copper key. She held it up and turned it around. "Pretty, isn't it? I told him where to look, but he had to do the work. He's really been very good at following directions, and he made it quite easy for me to set up light housekeeping across the street. But, alas, that is all over and done with. You played right into my hands as I thought you would. Did you *really* think you had defeated me, you foolish old biddy? You merely hastened the Day of Judgment. And it is at hand. My Lord and master is coming to meet us. And when he arrives it will be a very different world. *Very* different, I assure you. Let me see . . . you two will change first, I think." She pointed at Jonathan and then at Mrs. Zimmermann. "Yes, that's the way it will be. You two first, so Sonny here can watch. You'll want to watch, won't you, Lewis?"

Lewis stood with his back to Mrs. Izard. He was as still as a clothes-store dummy.

"Turn around, Lewis," said Mrs. Izard, in that nasty-sweet voice she had used from the beginning. "Don't you want to kiss your old Auntie Izard?"

He didn't move.

"Come now, Lewis. I command you. Don't be foolish. It'll just make things worse for you in the end. Turn around, I say!"

Lewis's body grew tense, and then he rushed forward into the tunnel. He picked up the clock, which had just begun to make that whirring sound clocks make when they are going to strike the hour.

"Stop, boy!" shouted Mrs. Izard. "Stop, you filthy fat

pig! I'll turn you into something that your own mother wouldn't—don't you dare! Don't . . . ."

Lewis threw the clock down. There was a sproinging of uncoiled springs and a clatter of cogs and a splintering of wood and a tinkle of broken glass. He reached down into the wreckage and ripped the pendulum free of the works, which were still buzzing furiously. At that moment, a figure which stood only a few yards from Lewis, the figure of an elderly man in a rotting black Sunday suit, vanished. Then there was an awful shriek, a loud, inhuman sound like a siren at the top of its wail. It filled the air and seemed to turn it red. Lewis covered his ears, but the sound was inside his head and in the marrow of his bones. And then it was gone.

He turned around. There stood Jonathan, smiling and trying to blink away the tears in his eyes. There stood Mrs. Zimmermann, smiling even more broadly. And behind them, on the cellar floor, under a swaying bare bulb, lay a crumpled pile of black cloth. A yellow skull was staring up out of it, staring up in gap-jawed amazement. A few wisps of gray hair clung to the crevices in the smooth dome, and over the empty eyeholes a pair of rimless glasses was perched. The glasses were shattered.

CHAPTER ELEVEN

Three days after the destruction of Mrs. Izard and her magic clock, Jonathan, Mrs. Zimmermann, and Lewis were sitting around a bonfire in the driveway of the house at 100 High Street. It was a chilly night, and the stars were cold overhead, but the fire burned a warm, bright orange. Mrs. Zimmermann had a steaming earthenware pot of cocoa by her side. She kept it close to the fire so it would stay warm. Jonathan and Lewis stared at the fire and sipped cocoa from their mugs. It tasted very good.

There was a pile of Isaac Izard's dusty papers in Jonathan's lap. Every now and then he would pick one up and throw it into the fire. Lewis watched each sheet as the fire licked at its corners, then blackened it, then wadded it into a fluffy ball of ashes.

After a while Lewis said, "Uncle Jonathan?"

"Yes, Lewis?"

"Was Mrs. Izard really trying to make the world end?"

"As far as I can tell, she was," said Jonathan. "And she would have done it, too, if you hadn't fixed her clock for her. But tell me, Lewis. Why didn't you turn around when we did?"

Lewis smiled broadly. "I looked at the glass door on the clock and I saw the reflection of what Mrs. Izard was holding, and I knew it was a Hand of Glory. John L. Stoddard tells you all about Hands of Glory."

"I'm glad he does," said Mrs. Zimmermann. "One look at that hand and you'd have been as numb as we were. But still, it took a great deal of courage for you to rush in and smash the clock. After all, you didn't know what would happen to you when you did that."

Lewis was silent. He had always thought that courage had something to do with riding your bicycle through bonfires and hanging by your knees from the limbs of trees.

Mrs. Zimmermann picked up a plate of chocolate-chip cookies and passed them around. Jonathan took two and Lewis took several. There was another silence while everyone munched and sipped for a while. Jonathan threw more papers into the fire.

Lewis squirmed around and stared at the dark house across the street.

"Do you think Mrs. Izard could ever . . . come back?" he said in a faltering voice.

"No," said Jonathan, shaking his head gravely. "No, Lewis, I think that when you smashed the clock in the walls, you destroyed any power she might have in this world. Just to be on the safe side, though, I put what was left of her back in the mausoleum and locked the doors with a nice shiny new lock. A lock that has had spells said over it. That ought to hold her for a while."

"What about the Hanchetts?" said Lewis. "I mean, are they going to come back to live in their house?"

Jonathan paused for a minute before speaking. He clicked the paper clips on his watch chain. "I think they are," he said at last. "But certain rites will have to be performed before they return. When an unclean spirit inhabits a house, it leaves behind a bad aura."

"Speaking of bad auras and unclean spirits," said Mrs. Zimmermann, "do you have any idea of what happened to Hammerhandle?"

Jonathan's face grew grim for an instant. He had made a few guesses about Hammerhandle's fate, but he had kept them to himself. For one thing, he knew that the blood of a hanged man went into the making of a Hand of Glory.

"No idea at all," said Jonathan, shaking his head. "He seems to have vanished from the face of the earth."

Suddenly Lewis began to squirm and scrunch around in his seat again. He was on the brink of saying something.

"Uncle . . . Jonathan?" Lewis's voice was dry and throaty.

"Yes, Lewis? What is it?"

"I . . . I let Mrs. Izard out of her tomb."

Jonathan smiled calmly. "Yes," he said. "I knew you did."

Lewis's mouth dropped open. "How did you know?"

"You left your flashlight up at the cemetery. I found it in a pile of leaves when I went up to put Mrs. Izard back in her tomb."

"Are you going to send me to the Detention Home?" asked Lewis in a tiny, frightened voice.

"Am I going to *what?*" said Jonathan, staring at him in disbelief. "Lewis, what kind of ogre do you think I am?

"And besides," Jonathan added with a sudden smile, "why should I punish you for doing what I tried to do myself when I was a boy? Like you, I was interested in magic at an early age. It runs in our family, I guess. I was trying to impress a girl. You wanted to keep Tarby for a friend. Isn't that right?"

Lewis nodded sadly.

"By the way, Lewis," said Mrs. Zimmermann. "How are things between you and Tarby these days?"

"Not so good," said Lewis. "I don't think Tarby and

I were meant to be friends. We're not the same type. But it doesn't matter."

"Doesn't matter?" said Jonathan. "Well, it certainly *does* matter! If he's such a stuck-up little . . ." He stopped because he saw that Lewis was smiling smugly.

Jonathan wrinkled up his eyebrows so that they looked like two mating auburn caterpillars. "Lewis Barnavelt!" he roared. "Are you hiding something from me?"

Lewis was trying very hard to keep from giggling. "Oh, nothing much, Uncle Jonathan," he said. "Except that I have a new friend."

"*Whaaat? You dooo?*" said Jonathan and Mrs. Zimmermann in unison.

"Yes. Her name is Rose Rita Pottinger, and she lives down on Mansion Street. She knows the names of all the different kinds of cannon. Want to hear them? Saker, minion, falconet, demi-culverin . . ."

"Aaaaah!" screamed Jonathan. He threw two fistfuls of paper into the fire. "That's all I need. An expert in Elizabethan ordnance. Promise me one thing, Lewis."

"What's that?"

"If you and tiny Rosie decide to start a cannon foundry in our basement, let Mrs. Zimmermann and me know so we can go visit my relatives in Osee Five Hills. Okay?"

Lewis giggled. "Sure, Uncle Jonathan. I'll let you know."

Jonathan waved his pipe at the bonfire. The leaves stirred uneasily, and then they gathered into a large black ball. The bonfire turned into a jack-o'-lantern. Now the three of them took turns pitching chestnuts into the eyes, nose, and mouth of the ferocious lantern. *Pop! Pop! Pop!* The chestnuts went off in a ripping string, like a fusillade of musket fire.

Jonathan, Lewis, and Mrs. Zimmermann sat around the fire talking until the scowling orange face fell in with an airy *whoosh*. Then they got up, stretched, and went wearily off to bed.

About the Author

John Bellairs was the critically acclaimed, best-selling author of many Gothic novels: *The Curse of the Blue Figurine, The Mummy, the Will, and the Crypt, The Lamp from the Warlock's Tomb, The Spell of the Sorcerer's Skull, The Revenge of the Wizard's Ghost, The Chessmen of Doom, The Eyes of the Killer Robot,* and the novels starring Lewis Barnavelt, Rose Rita Pottinger, and Mrs. Zimmermann — *The House with a Clock in Its Walls, The Figure in the Shadows, The Letter, the Witch, and the Ring,* and *The Ghost in the Mirror* (completed by Brad Strickland).

John Bellairs died in 1991. However, there are several more books that Mr. Bellairs left that Puffin will be publishing. Brad Strickland, a longtime Bellairs fan, will be completing them, just as he did *The Ghost in the Mirror*.

About the Artist

Edward Gorey is the well-known illustrator of many books, including *The Shrinking of Treehorn* and *Sam and Emma*, both selected for the 1972 Children's Book Showcase, and *Red Riding Hood*. He lives in New York City.

The text of this book was set in Janson, a Linotype face based on the original design of Antonius Janson, a Dutch punchcutter and typefounder who worked in Frankfurt and Leipzig from 1651 to 1687. The Linotype rendition of Janson, introduced in 1932, was cut by the Mergenthaler Linotype Company under the direction of C. H. Griffith. Janson is an old style book face characterized by narrow characters and a marked contrast between thick and thin strokes.

Composition by Connecticut Printers, Inc.

Typography by Atha Tehon